Knight's Storm

Sanctuary Falls, Book 1

Katie Reus

Prologue

"Can I get your phone number?" Nick Storm hadn't asked for a woman's number in… He couldn't even remember. But as he stood there covered in hot coffee, he wasn't letting this chance go.

The woman, Berkley, smiled up at him, and he didn't care that moments before she'd spilled coffee on him.

He wasn't letting on that it burned because it was clear she felt bad enough. And her smile was like the sun coming out.

"Oh my god, of course. But I can just pay you for the dry cleaning now. You don't have to hunt me down for it, promise." She shook her head slightly, her dark hair swishing around her shoulders. "I seriously can't believe I did that. I wasn't paying attention. Clearly," she added, with another light laugh. She was carrying two big bags, one filled with what looked like random fabric and another that was zipped up so he couldn't see inside. The front of it said *So Many Books, So Little Time.*

"So who's the 'adorable assface' you were talking to?" he asked.

"Oh my god, you heard that? It's my youngest brother. And he *is* an adorable assface."

He laughed at her horrified expression, her green eyes wide as she talked about her brother.

"I have a younger sister so I get the frustration." He cleared his throat. "Also, I'm asking for your number because I would like to take you out. On a date." He wanted that really clear. "I wasn't asking because I want you to pay for dry cleaning." Or anything else. Because yeah, he needed to get this shirt off as soon as he got out of here. He probably also needed to put Neosporin or something on his chest too.

"Oh." Now she blinked up at him, looking unsure.

Maybe he'd misread the vibe between them. Or maybe she wasn't single. She didn't have a ring on but that didn't mean anything. She could be in a committed relationship, or hell, just not into him.

"Okay," she finally said after what was only a second, but for some reason felt like a season had passed.

He cleared his throat. "It's okay. I'm not trying to pressure you. We're good, I promise."

"No," she blurted. "It's not that. I just... You know what, yes, you can have my phone number." She smiled again in that same warm way as before and he felt it all the way to his core.

He couldn't ever remember being this affected by a woman, and definitely not someone he'd just met. Something about her smile was infectious though and he found himself wanting to smile right back at her.

"Fair warning, I've been out of the game a while and have limited social skills," she said as she pulled out her phone.

Which made him laugh. "My sister tells me that my social skills suck too, so we've already got that in common."

She laughed a little harder, then rattled off her number. He texted her so she'd have his number and then he lost track of time as they made small talk outside the coffee shop—until she got a phone call and had to leave.

He needed to get to work too, but hadn't cared about being late for his morning meeting. Because something told him that his life had just changed.

"Nick."

He glanced over to see Henry Moore walking up to the coffee shop. He shouldn't be surprised since it was across the street from the hospital. Made sense the surgeon would frequent it. "Hey. How are you?"

"Good. Tired of the cafeteria food so sneaking out for a bit." His smile was easy, but shifted ever so slightly. "Did I just see you talking to my ex-wife?"

He hadn't even realized Henry had been married. Nick had been in the man's office a couple times for post-op discussions with his sister, but he'd had absolutely nothing personal in there except a few awards and framed pictures of himself accepting said awards. "I was talking to a woman named Berkley."

"That's her. Best and worst years of my life," he said on a laugh that sounded more strained than anything. "If she hadn't cheated on me, I'd have forgiven her for anything." Now he shook his head slightly, looking almost defeated. But then he clapped Nick's shoulder once and seemed to force a smile. Something Nick had seen his own mother do time and time again after his dad cheated on her. "I've got to get in there before the line gets too long, but I'll see you soon. We'll catch up."

He nodded and murmured something polite, but that high he'd been feeling cracked and fizzled. Part of him hated that he'd run into Henry, but he'd rather know the truth now than later.

Henry had saved his sister's life, was one of the best surgeons on the East Coast, had dedicated his life to helping others. And the pain in his voice had been real.

Sighing, he deleted Berkley Knight's phone number from his cell so he wouldn't be tempted to reach out to her. He knew what a destructive wake cheaters left and he wanted no part of it.

Chapter 1

"SORRY I'M LATE." BERKLEY slid onto the barstool next to Silvia, one of her oldest friends.

"You're not late. I'm early." Silvia held up a glass of dark red wine, the color similar to her hair. "And I started without you."

"I'm actually only drinking sparkling water tonight. I've got to wake up early. But I am starving." She glanced down at the short bar menu even though she knew what she was going to order—bang bang shrimp. "So how was your day?" She set the menu back down, wincing a little at the stickiness.

The End Zone was one of her favorite places in Sanctuary Falls but they could stand to clean up a bit more. Something she never would have noticed a few years ago.

"Long. This new job is... I can't talk about it just yet, but it's a pain in the ass." Sighing, Silvia took a sip of her wine. "It doesn't even matter. I'm just happy to see you." She glanced at her cell. "Kendall should be here soon too."

"She said she had big work news." Berkley was so happy for her. Both she and Kendall had struggled in their early twenties, partied too much and made a lot of mistakes. But they'd both turned things around and Kendall deserved all the good things.

Silvia's expression was oddly neutral.

"What?" Berkley asked, wondering how bad this new job was. Silvia was a private investigator, and while she took independent jobs, she also took contract work from insurance companies or law firms. Berkley guessed this was one of those jobs.

"Nothing. Just…" She cleared her throat, was just starting to say something when Kendall slid up to the table, a big smile on her face as she shed her puffer jacket.

January in North Carolina required it.

"Hey guys." Kendall set two little gift bags on the round table, but paused as their server came up and took the rest of their order. "Water, really? It's Friday." Her tone was light, taking the sting out of her words.

"I know, I'm getting up early," Berkley said.

"I don't know how you do that bouldering stuff." She shook her head.

Berkley had started bouldering a few months ago, and to her surprise, loved it. She'd always been into hiking, but climbing scared her. Bouldering was a lot different though and she liked how much it kept her focused. Since getting her life back on track, she'd found hobbies she loved in addition to a job she loved. It made a big difference in her outlook on life. "One move at a time."

Kendall snorted. "You're such a nerd. Now open your presents."

Silvia made a little oohing sound as she pulled out a travel-size perfume bottle and Berkley found the same but travel-sized lotions.

"Thank you, these are great… What's this for though?" Berkley asked.

Kendall shrugged, tossing her long, white-blonde hair over her shoulder—and Berkley didn't miss the double take one of the men at the table behind them gave her. Soon she'd be getting drinks sent over. It always happened.

"My dermatologist had a basket of leftover stuff today, so I snagged a bunch for you guys."

Silvia laughed lightly. "I need to change dermatologists."

"Right? Thanks, Kendall. This is really sweet." She was always bringing them little gifts. "So, what's your big news?"

"Oh." Her face fell. "Nothing. I was up for shift supervisor, but it didn't work out."

"Is it because of...Henry?" She hated that she even had to ask. Berkley's ex-husband was a very talented neurosurgeon at the same hospital Kendall worked at and she swore he just loved making anyone in her orbit miserable.

Another shrug. "I honestly don't know. He has a lot of sway, but...if it is because of him, I could never prove it."

Yet another way her shitty ex screwed with her life—by hurting the people she loved.

She'd never hated another person the way she hated him. Hell, she hadn't thought it possible to loathe someone that much. She didn't want to loathe him, she just wanted to move on from him and be done. It wasn't like they had kids or anything, but Henry kept shoving himself back into her orbit in little ways that tested all her patience. She wished he would just move on. "I know it's not my fault, but I'm still sorry."

"It's definitely not your fault," Silvia added in a hard tone. "He's a dick. I'm sorry about the job though, Kendall. That sucks."

"It's fine. I love being a nurse. And I'm thinking about looking into travel nursing, maybe for just a year or two. The money is so good and I could build up a nice nest egg and get more experience."

"I love that..." Berkley trailed off as her charming, unfortunately good-looking ex strolled into the bar. He made eye contact before she could look away. "Speak of the devil," she muttered. *Come on universe! Give me a break.*

"Hello, ladies." He stopped at their high-top table, gave Kendall what Berkley could only describe as a lecherous grin. "You're all looking...fit."

Ew. Ew, ew, ew. How had she married this tool? He'd put on such a good mask. Hell, a perfect one. He'd reeled her in and it wasn't until months after they were married that he'd shown his true colors.

"And you're looking gross. Go away," Silvia responded before Berkley could find her voice.

His expression chilled considerably as he turned to Silvia—who had never liked him. He gave her an icy smile, then turned that faux charm on Berkley that had stopped working years ago.

"How was your Christmas?" he asked.

"Great, thanks." She kept her tone as neutral as possible, even as she wished she could just ignore him. But there were people she knew in this bar and she had no doubt they were watching their interaction with interest. She refused to give them anything to talk about or post on social media. She wasn't the mess she'd been before marrying Henry. Hell, part of the reason she'd married him—something she could only see in hindsight—was because she'd thought he was good for her, would help turn around her reputation.

He nodded and she could see a hint of the old cruelty glint in his dark eyes. "That's great. I hear your little business is doing well now too. I'm so happy you landed on your feet—though I'm sure that settlement from me didn't hurt any." He laughed loudly, and she couldn't even fake a smile.

Instead she picked up her water and focused on drinking it as if it was the most important thing in the world. Sure, she could snap back at him, but that was what he wanted. A reaction. And she refused to give him one, especially in front of all these curious stares.

"Scram," Silvia said as both she and Kendall remained quiet.

"Did you just say...scram?" Henry blinked at her, incredulous.

"Would *get lost* work better for you? Or how about 'get thee from my sight'? Ooh, or what about 'depart, demon'?" Silvia nodded, clearly pleased with herself. "That one works on a couple levels, because I'm not convinced you're not at least part demon."

"There's something seriously wrong with you," he muttered before stalking away, headed...

Berkley didn't even care where he was going. She was just glad he was gone, so she turned away, focusing on her friends as she snickered. "Thank you."

Kendall laughed too. "God, I hate that man."

Silvia just shrugged, but she looked pleased with herself. "What are friends for?"

Berkley's chest warmed at her friend's nonchalant answer because she was so damn grateful for the two of them. They'd been there for her in a big way after her divorce. And when Henry had made a move on Kendall, she'd shut him down fast. Now Berkley was pretty sure it was coming back to haunt her friend at work. Tale as old as time with men in power.

She'd told her friend that she needed to file a report with HR, but Kendall wasn't interested in that. He was the hospital's star surgeon and beloved by a whole lot of people. Everyone knew he'd slept around with half the nurses.

Everyone but her, apparently. And no one cared or did anything about it. The man was untouchable.

Whatever, she wasn't going to waste any more time thinking about him. She'd divorced him two years ago, had officially moved on, and the last year had been one of her best.

She refused to give him any more space in her head.

Even though her gut reaction was to order a stronger drink, she stuck with water. Because that was the old Berkley just wanting to react. She wasn't going to let him or anyone control her actions anymore.

***

Groaning, Berkley opened her eyes and rolled over... "What the hell?" She pushed up on the chilled tile floor, blinking as she glanced around the unfamiliar surroundings.

A dull ache thumped at the back of her skull as she sat fully up, tried to figure out what was going on.

She was in...a kitchen she didn't recognize. Stove, microwave above it, top-of-the-line refrigerator. Definitely not her kitchen.

Reaching up, she gently touched the back of her head, felt a knot. Winced.

The last thing she remembered was leaving the bar last night. She'd had to park in the back, and by the time she left she'd been cursing to herself about letting her friends leave before her—because she'd had to walk to her Bronco by herself.

Feeling almost hungover, she managed to get to her feet, stumbled into the countertop, managed to steady herself. She knew she hadn't been drunk but...her head throbbed.

She was still dressed at least, as a new fear settled in her bones. Looking around the pristine kitchen she didn't see her purse or phone or...anything of hers. And she was still wearing her shoes and jacket.

She took a tentative step forward, wobbled a little. "Hello?" Her throat was dry. Immediately she stopped herself. What if someone had abducted her? She wasn't tied up or anything but...something was very, very wrong.

As a wave of nausea swept through her, she paused against the granite countertop, steadied herself again.

The blinds in the kitchen were closed, but enough light was coming through them that she knew it was early morning. Maybe sunrise.

She needed a clock.

She scanned the room, saw the time was five forty-five. She'd been out for hours. Where was she, and how had she gotten here?

Another wave of dread swept through her, but she forced her feet to keep moving as she stumbled through the house. Living room empty, bedroom empty, office empty...

She sucked in a breath as she spotted the body lying dead still in the middle of a king-sized bed. She couldn't actually see a wound of any kind, but the man's face was slack, unmoving, and had a sick pallor. He had to be dead.

Swallowing hard, she stumbled back once, went to grip the doorframe but stopped herself.

She was in the house with a dead man and no memory of how she'd gotten here. She couldn't leave fingerprints.

Because there was no way in hell she was calling the cops. Not with her history.

Even as fear spiked through her, everything still fuzzy, she retreated out of the room and made her way back to the living room where she'd seen a landline.

With trembling fingers, she slid on the mittens in her pocket then dialed a number she had memorized. A burner phone she knew she could call day or night.

"Yeah?" Her youngest brother answered on the first ring, sounding wide-awake.

"Micah," she whispered, shoving down the rising panic. "I think I'm in trouble."

Chapter 2

"Do not touch anything," Micah ordered, no give in his voice.

"I've only touched a few things," Berkley said, even as she grabbed a dishrag from one of the drawers in the kitchen. Then she promptly wiped down the doorknob. Even with her mittens on, she was wiping anything and everything, even the landline phone. "That I remember."

"I'm tracking the number you called from now." He was silent for a few beats. "You know a guy named James Reed?"

"No. Or I don't think so." Her head still ached as fear threatened to overwhelm her. "I can't think," she rasped out, panic punching through her. "But I didn't drink last night! I didn't do this. I swear I didn't tie one on and—"

"I believe you." Micah's quiet voice cut through what was surely about to be a panicked tirade.

She pulled in a breath, then counted to five. His quick response settled something inside her. "Okay, thank you. And no, I don't think I know that name, but I couldn't swear to it."

"I'm only twenty minutes away, so sit tight. And don't go outside, in case this place has cameras or the neighbors do."

Which they likely did. Everyone had cameras now, at least doorbell ones. Which meant...someone might have seen her arriving last night. Or being carried in? Because she didn't think she'd walked in here of her own volition.

As she waited for her brother, she started wiping down every spot she knew she'd touched. Was she contaminating a crime scene? Yes. But she knew that if she called the cops, she'd be hauled in and likely charged in the murder of the random man in the other room.

She'd made a lot of bad (mostly alcohol-fueled) decisions when she was younger, and her past would absolutely come back to haunt her. Because while she believed in second chances, the law certainly didn't.

So she wasn't going to stick around and let the cops decide she was guilty. Intellectually she knew that not all of law enforcement would paint her with the same brush but... She paused at a slight sound, tensed.

"Berkley?" Micah's whisper carried from the back of the house.

"In the kitchen." She didn't want to leave the room and deposit more forensic evidence around.

Sanctuary Falls had a decent-sized sheriff's department with at least two solid detectives that she knew of. One in particular was a bulldog. She had to be careful right now.

Her brother stepped into the room wearing a ball cap pulled over what looked like a wig, given the longer reddish hair sticking out, as well as a surgical-style mask. He held out gloves. "Put these on and show me where he is. Then we're going to go over what you remember."

In the bedroom, he was careful as he stepped inside. And that was when she saw the dark-colored booties slipped over his shoes.

She wanted to turn away, but considering he was here doing her a favor, she made herself watch as he inspected the...body. The room was freezing. Actually the whole house was, something she was belatedly realizing.

"He's been stabbed," Micah said into the quiet.

She almost jumped, but simply nodded. "Is there a weapon or anything around?"

He moved quickly, ducking down to look under the bed then looking around the room with efficient precision. As if he'd done this type of thing before. Which for all she knew, he had. Her brother had...interesting friends.

Or contacts, as he liked to say. And she knew he'd taken contract jobs that were in a gray area. None of the family knew precisely what he did for a living, just that he "made problems go away" or as he liked to tell them, he was an "analyst" which was such bullshit. He was gone for weeks at a time with no contact, but whenever she'd needed him, Micah was always there.

"I don't see anything here, but that doesn't mean it's not in the house."

"Where was he stabbed?" she asked, stepping into the room again. She picked up a wallet tossed onto the dresser and thumbed through it with her gloved fingers. She found his ID and held it up as her brother approached.

Micah snapped a picture with a burner phone. "Right in the side of the neck. The wound is small and he might have other damage, but that's the one I can see without moving the covers too much."

She nodded, fighting another wave of nausea. She wasn't sure if it was from her head injury or the thought of the dead man lying only a few feet away. Now that she had a better angle, she could see the blood soaking through the sheet and likely beyond to the mattress.

"Same name as the owner of the house. James Reed." Micah frowned at the ID, then looked around the room with a critical eye.

She did the same even as the back of her skull pounded with each second that passed. She must have winced or made a face because her brother aimed his frown at her.

"Look at me."

"I am looking at you."

He narrowed his gaze as he stared into her eyes. Then he said, "Turn around." When she did, he gently touched the back of her head.

She jerked away even as he said, "I'm taking you to the hospital."

"No way. I'm fine."

"I think you might have a concussion. Do you feel nauseous? Dizzy?"

"I have a headache...because someone hit me on the back of the head. And fine, I feel lightheaded. But I'm not going anywhere. I was at The End Zone last night. That's the last thing I remember. I want to see if my Bronco is still there. And my phone. I need to figure out what happened. I'm not calling the cops. And you know why." She gave him a hard look.

"Yeah, that'll just open up a mess neither of us want to deal with. Fine, but I'm reserving the right to take you to the walk-in clinic if I think you need it. Or I have a doctor friend I could ask for a favor, but I want to save that one for if we really need it."

"Deal. Also…what are we doing about this?" She couldn't bring herself to say *the body* or the guy's name. Berkley knew in her bones that she hadn't stabbed some stranger, but she was still trying to disconnect from this.

"I saw he's got a home office in one of the rooms so I'm going to check it out and see if I can find anything on his computer. I want you to stand in the kitchen and do nothing."

"I haven't looked in the garage yet. I'll do that while you're in his office." Because she couldn't just stand around. "Also we need to grab Tylenol or something when we leave." She paused at a sound from outside, her fear spiking when she thought it was a siren. But nope, just a horn beep indicating someone had locked their vehicle.

Which reminded her she needed to ask Micah how he'd gotten here, or more specifically where he'd parked. But that was a question for later.

"Fine, but be careful."

She kept her gloves on as she stepped into his laundry room, then into the garage. It was a generous sized two-car with one vehicle inside. A four-door sedan—

"Hey, let's go."

She turned at her brother's voice, winced at the sudden move but bit it back so he wouldn't see. "You find anything?"

"Maybe." His expression was almost pensive but she couldn't get a solid read on him before he turned away.

So she followed even as the invisible weight on her shoulders grew heavier.

***

"Are you going to get out?" Micah asked her as they sat in his idling vehicle.

After leaving the dead man's house, he'd driven her to the bar from the night before. The End Zone opened soon for lunch but there weren't many vehicles in the parking lot.

Just hers and two others.

"Yeah. I'm just...I don't know. Processing everything." And fine, she didn't want to get out of his truck because once she did, the real world would crash back on her. In Micah's warm truck, she was just the middle sister with her younger brother and she could pretend that everything was okay.

Or not.

She slid out of his truck before she could change her mind and zipped up her jacket as she approached her Bronco. She tried the handle, and to her surprise, it opened. Her keys were tossed onto the passenger seat. And her purse was on the passenger-side floorboard. "Weird," she muttered more to herself even though she'd heard her brother get out and approach.

"This yours?" He bent down and reached under the SUV to pull out her cell.

"Yeah." She opened it, saw she had a handful of missed calls and texts. Ignored them all for now. Scrubbing a hand over her face, she glanced around. "This place has to have security cameras. Right?" Everywhere seemed to nowadays.

James Reed's home only had a doorbell camera and Micah had been quiet about what he'd found on the guy's computer. Because she knew when her brother was holding something back.

Now wasn't the time to push though.

"Let's find out."

She grabbed her keys and locked her vehicle before hurrying after him. Damn it, she really did need something for her headache.

Inside they were greeted by the familiar scent of fried food and a much darker atmosphere, which she appreciated at the moment.

"Hey, two of my favorite Knights." Will Gillis was behind the bar, a towel tucked into his pants, a tablet in his hand as he took inventory. "We're not serving food for another half hour."

"Oh, I know." Berkley managed to smile as she approached the bar top and sat down. He was acting normal so she must have not done anything stupid in here last night. Which would have been one of her fears a decade ago—that she'd gotten drunk, made a fool of herself and couldn't remember who she'd pissed off.

To be fair, she hadn't normally pissed people off, she'd just been drunk and up for anything. And a bit mischievous.

Okay, she'd been a full-on menace who had once thought it was a great idea to break into a gas station one town over after hours because they had the candy she wanted. No one actually knew about that one and she was forever grateful. Kinda the way she was grateful that no one but her closest girlfriends knew she'd once taken a bread truck on a joyride because the driver had left the keys in it. (To be fair, she'd gassed it up and returned it later). "I'm just looking for my phone, thought I might have left it in here last night."

"I'm gonna hit the head, be back in a second." Micah leaned over the bar and clapped hands with Will in that way guys seemed to be born knowing how to do. They'd been in the same graduating class in high school and everyone loved Micah. Will too, for that matter.

"See ya in a sec. And if you did leave your phone, it's in here." Will pulled out a basket and set it on the bar. "So, you here to pay your friend's tab?"

"Friend?"

"Blondie. I forget her name."

Damn it. "Kendall didn't pay her bill?"

He lifted a shoulder, seeming unconcerned. "She left cash but it wasn't enough to cover her last couple shots."

Ah. "You sure someone didn't grab her money?" Berkley asked as she pulled out her wallet, glad that no one had stolen her vehicle or purse. Nope, someone had stolen time from her and tried to set her up for murder, or at least indicate that she was involved in it, and that was a hell of a lot worse. "Maybe check the cameras?"

"Cameras are for back here," he muttered, motioning to the bar. "To make sure we don't steal." He rolled his eyes. "And no one took her cash. She handed it to me but I didn't count it until later."

"How much does she owe you?"

"You're not covering—"

"Yeah, I am. I'll grab the difference from her later. I don't want your till to be short."

Now he gave her a big grin, revealing a hidden dimple. "There's a reason I love you Knights."

"Yeah, yeah." She made small talk for another five minutes until her brother came out, gave her a small nod, indicating he must have slipped into the back office and gotten what he needed from the security cameras.

She'd find out soon enough anyway.

After another ten minutes of more small talk, she and her brother finally made their escape outside. "So?" she demanded as they approached his truck. "What did you find?"

Micah had started to respond when an unmarked Explorer zoomed into the gravel parking lot, blue lights flashing.

Oh god.

Chapter 3

BERKLEY DIDN'T REALIZE SHE was holding her breath until her sister Krystal stepped out of her unmarked sheriff's department SUV. Even so, a cold shiver snaked down her spine. Her sister wasn't coming to arrest her, right? Wouldn't be the first time, sadly.

She resisted the urge to look at Micah—no way he'd called Krystal. Right?

But then Krystal's big grin unclenched her stomach and made her realize everything was fine.

"Hey, you two. You guys grabbing lunch?"

"Ah, no, just paying a bill at the bar," Micah answered smoothly. It wasn't a lie either, which soothed her conscience.

"Gotcha." Krystal wasn't in full uniform. As a recently promoted detective, she was usually in "casual detective wear" as Berkley liked to think of it. Right now that was jeans and a Sanctuary Falls PD green wool pullover that matched her eyes. The Knight siblings all had varying shades of green eyes. "I missed breakfast so I might sneak in there and see if Will can convince the cook to make me something."

"You know he will," Berkley said. Her sister was probably a decade-ish older than the bartender but she was also sure the guy had a crush on her. A lot of people did. And who could blame them? Former homecoming and prom queen who'd basically raised her siblings and was now a badass detective? It was hard not to look up to her. Berkely certainly did, and couldn't stand the thought of disappointing her sister again.

"Have you guys heard from Apollo? I've been texting him and he's leaving his messages unread." Her expression was neutral enough, but Berkley knew her sister was worried, could see it in her eyes.

Berkley shook her head. "I haven't talked to him. But I'm sure that's not a surprise." She loved her oldest brother, but they weren't tight the way she and Micah were. Whereas Krystal and Apollo were barely a year apart and basically besties. Cormac was smack dab in the middle of all of them and he was good about staying in touch with everyone.

"He hasn't responded to my texts either," Micah said.

Krystal narrowed her gaze at him. "That's not actually an answer and I know how sneaky you are. Have you talked to him on the phone in the last twenty-four hours? Or in person?"

Micah blinked, and oh, Berkley realized that he *had* talked to their brother because the truth was written all over his face. (It was hard to lie to Krystal when she'd been a mother to all of them after their own had been murdered.)

Krystal opened her mouth to say something, but then her radio went off and she answered the call. Then turned to them, gave Micah a pointed look. "This isn't over."

"Love you," was his response as she hurried back to her SUV.

"Should we tell her what happened?" Berkley blurted as their sister zoomed off. She knew the answer was no, but still.

He was shaking his head before she finished the question. "Hell no. She'll be obligated to do something about it. And if she doesn't, the guilt will eat away at her. If you tell her and ask her to keep it a secret, it puts her in an unwinnable position. You're doing her a favor by keeping this a secret."

"Fine...you're probably not wrong. I know I can't tell her, I just..."

"Don't like lying to her. I know."

"So what's up with Apollo?"

"We don't have time to talk about that. I made a copy of the bar's security feeds from last night. I only scanned a couple frames and they're all disappointing but let's get in my truck and see if there's anything that'll help us figure out what happened to you last night."

Her stomach tightened, but she nodded and got into his truck. She wanted to see what had happened, but part of her was scared of the outcome.

"I'm forwarding to the time frame you remember so we can see—hopefully—when you left."

She felt her phone buzzing in her pocket, but ignored it. She was supposed to have lunch with Silvia and Kendall but was thinking of blowing them off. She wasn't in the right headspace for anything right now, but definitely not casual conversation.

"There I am. You can see me moving in the reflection of the mirror behind the bar." She squinted as if that would help her see better, but all she saw was herself packing up her purse, saying good-bye to some people she hadn't seen in ages, then leaving.

"And here you are outside." Her brother's tone was frustrated. "For just a second, then…" He pulled up another file, then cursed. "It's ridiculous that they only have two cameras outside and both have shitty angles. Right at the front door and then one facing the dumpster," he muttered.

"Will said that the interior cameras are only facing the actual bar. Clearly the owner only cares about getting stolen from. Or…I don't know, I guess catching people who use his dumpster too?" What a tool. Her phone buzzed again and this time Micah looked up.

"Who keeps texting you?" he asked.

"Just the girls. I'm supposed to meet them at Brunch and Bliss." One of their favorite spots.

"Good. Go meet them, and I'm going to be digging into Reed's computer files."

Not that she needed the reminder that he was dead, but his name still jarred her. "No, I think I'll go home and..." What? Take a shower? Wash off last night?

"Well you should definitely go home, but just to freshen up and change—and we need to dump your clothes. I'll burn everything. You need to talk to Silvia and Kendall, find out if they know anything. We're trying to piece together last night. And whatever you do, *don't* tell them what happened. We've got to keep this circle tight."

Yeah, she knew that even if she hated it. "Fine. You're right."

"Words I can never hear enough."

She nudged him once, then sobered. "Listen, thank you for—"

"Nope, not doing this. You don't thank me for this. We're family...and you've never judged me for anything."

True enough. She knew her brother lived in shades of gray, and if anything, she was a little in awe of him. He lived life by his own rules and made no apologies. "Fine, but thank you anyway," she rushed out before she exited the truck.

It was time to put her game face on and hopefully get some answers.

***

"So, tell us about the guy you left with," Silvia said to Kendall, who'd arrived ten minutes later than Berkley.

She'd been so worried about running late, but as per usual, Kendall was later than all of them. And all their texts had just been fun memes and normal talk, nothing serious.

Silvia had been normal when she'd arrived, so clearly she didn't know that Berkley had left with—or been abducted by?—some random and now-dead guy last night. She really wanted to tell Silvia about it, get her advice, but her brother was right.

She had to keep the circle tight. Her friends needed plausible deniability anyway so she couldn't drag them into this.

Before Kendall could answer, their server set a small flight of different flavored mimosas on the table.

"Oh, we didn't order—"

"I ordered them on the way in," Kendall cut in. "Figured we could all indulge since we all have the same day off."

A rarity with the three of them. With Kendall being a nurse, Berkley working random days and hours, and Silvia's job as a private investigator with equally odd hours, she was right.

But Berkley only picked up a glass to be polite. She'd swish it around because no way was she drinking today. After being knocked out, she needed to keep a clear head. At this point she didn't think she had a concussion but...still. Better to be smart about things.

"We've actually been talking for a month," Kendall said, jumping right into it from Silvia's previous question.

And Berkley was grateful for it because she didn't have the energy for much small talk. But she could listen. And even though she'd thought she wasn't hungry, she ended up devouring a waffle board that was meant for two people.

Because it was definitely that kind of day.

When the bill came, the champagne flutes ended up on her tab even though she hadn't drunk any, but she didn't say anything. Just like she was never going to ask Kendall to pay her back for the drinks from last night.

"That's enough from me," Kendall said with a laugh once they'd all paid. "Who's the mystery man I saw you with in the parking lot last night?"

For a moment, Berkley froze as she was putting her wallet back in her purse, but then realized Kendall was looking at Silvia.

Who now had big cartoon eyes. "Ah, no one."

"Oooh, lies. I saw you talking with someone and you pretended you didn't hear me. I couldn't see their face though."

Berkley had still been inside when they'd left—had seen them both on the camera feed leaving. But she hadn't seen Silvia heading out with anyone.

Silvia lifted a shoulder, sniffed once. "I don't have to tell you two everything. I'm talking to someone and saw him last night."

It had been years since Silvia had dated, so this was definitely news. "Talking as in...dating?"

Silvia lifted the same shoulder, looking anything but relaxed. "I mean, yeah."

"How long?" Berkley asked.

"A month. Or two."

"Wait, two months? It's January... You were 'talking' to someone over the holidays? Did you guys exchange Christmas gifts?"

Silvia's cheeks flushed and she shrugged, but her face was a giveaway.

"Oh my go—"

Silvia stood abruptly, her cell in her hand. "I love you two, but I'm not talking about this. And I've gotta run anyway. My mom needs me to do a grocery run for her."

Berkley knew better than to push so she hugged her friend good-bye.

Once it was just the two of them, Kendall laughed. "Maybe he's an uggo and she doesn't want us to meet him."

"Hey." Berkley frowned at her.

But Kendall held up her palms. "I'm just playing. Silvia can get anyone she wants. I'm just nosy...and I've had one too many mimosas."

"You need a ride home?"

"No, I didn't drive."

Berkley knew she preferred to Uber and just nodded. "I need to use the restroom, but we'll talk later."

When she stepped back into the main room of the mint green and pink restaurant, Kendall was long gone, and their server was seating two familiar faces at the table they'd just been at. Just in time to grab something because the place closed at two.

Today of all days she had to run into Nick and Clover Storm. She actually liked the latter, but Nick...ugh.

She gave a warm smile to Clover, but had to mask her irritation at the sight of Clover's older brother Nick. Seriously, what a dumb name. Nick Storm. Sounded like a stupid, B-movie superhero.

Unfortunately, he was good-looking enough to be an A-list superhero. Their parents had made some ridiculously beautiful kids. Tall, athletic, looked as if they should be on ads for the latest winter sport.

Too bad Nick had the personality of a rock. Or toast.

The first time she'd met him—spilled coffee on him—he'd been open and warm, and whew, talk about giving her butterflies. The kind she'd only ever read about before. But then it was like he'd flipped a switch and turned into a... Maybe not an asshole, but at least an assface. It had been a year and she still remembered how he'd made her feel that day.

She gave him a bland not-really-a-smile before turning back to Clover with a real one. "Fun running into you here."

"I'm trying the waffle board you raved about." Clover grinned, her smile so warm and genuine it made it impossible for Berkley to not return it.

"You won't be disappointed. So we still on for tomorrow?" She hadn't heard any different, but right about now she needed to talk so they wouldn't lapse into any awkward pauses.

Because Nick was just staring straight ahead, not even looking at her. Nope, he rarely deigned to turn those gunmetal gray eyes on her. He was friendly with her ex-husband—who had saved Clover's life with emergency surgery—so she kind of understood why he was frosty to her.

But he was the one who'd asked for her number then just...not called. It wasn't like she'd ghosted him or anything. Now he acted as if she'd personally wronged him in life.

That was why it was a surprise that his sister had reached out to Berkley about a job.

And it was clearly a surprise to Nick because his head finally jerked up to look between them.

She refused to look at him again, just kept a smile in place as Clover nodded.

"Oh yeah. Livie Zamora is obsessed with the job you did for her, is telling everyone how amazing you are."

Berkley felt her cheeks flush under the praise, something she was still getting used to. She'd spent her younger years getting into trouble and was known for being the "wild Knight." Now she had a respectable job as owner of a full-service estate clean out company for larger homes. She handled everything from the cleanouts, right down to sorting and pricing items for online auctions. She even staged homes in the case people wanted to sell their home after a clean out. People who had once looked down on her treated her completely differently now.

She was grateful for the second chance and loved her job, but it was still surreal sometimes.

When she started to respond, Nick cleared his throat. "We need to order before they start closing down the kitchen."

Okay then, talk about a not-subtle hint. "Ah, right. I'll talk to you tomorrow." She still didn't look at him, just gave Clover a warm smile before heading out.

Cold rushed over her as she stepped out onto the sidewalk. At least the sun was bright, a nice balance to the iciness wrapping around her. And for a moment she could just focus on how much she wanted to wipe that stupid "I'm better than you" look off Nick Storm's face.

He and his perfect jawline, gorgeous cheekbones and eyelashes so thick she'd have probably sold part of her soul to have. A man that gorgeous was naturally a giant asshole. He loved his sister though, she'd give him that.

But that was all she'd give him.

Aaaand that was enough of that because she had way more important shit to worry about than some handsome asshole who got under her skin.

Like the dead guy whose home she'd woken up in that morning. Apparently no one had seen her leave with him. Or more likely be abducted by...him? Someone else?

There was no way she would have left all her stuff behind like that. Her keys, purse, phone... And the back of her skull still ached. So she'd definitely been either taken by him or someone else. But why? Other than the obvious.

But she hadn't been sexually assaulted. Or she was ninety-nine percent sure she hadn't been. Her clothes were still intact, she wasn't sore, and the biggest clue—she'd still had a tampon in when she'd gone to the bathroom after her brother had picked her up.

So why had she been in James Reed's home? Why was he dead? And who had killed him? And...was someone trying to frame her? Or implicate her?

She had no real enemies—except her ex-husband.

Chapter 4

"What's that look?" Nick asked even though he knew exactly what the look was.

"I hate the way you act when you're around Berkley. Or if I'm being honest, I kind of hate the way you are with some women in general." Clover sat back in her chair, her hard expression one he'd never seen.

"Wait, what?" He frowned at her, beyond surprised at not only her words, but her tight expression. She looked mad—at *him*.

"You're a hell of a lot harder on women than you are on men. And I kind of get it because our mom didn't protect us, but oh my god, Nick. You're turning into Dad." She blurted the words out in a rush, and whatever the server saw on his face made the woman turn right around and hurry away from them.

"I...am not." He cleared his throat, wondering what the hell was happening right now. They both hated their father. He'd been an abusive, cheating asshole, so any comparison to him... *What the hell.*

"Uh, yeah, you are. You do it in a hundred little ways. Not with me, but that's because you're way too overprotective. When Hannah left her husband because he was an abusive prick, the first thing you said was 'she should have picked better.' Not, 'her ex shouldn't have been an abusive prick.' And yeah, you helped her out financially and made sure she landed on her feet, but that judgment was still there. Even if you never said the words to her,

I can definitely see it in your expression. And deep down I keep wondering when you're going to judge me for doing something and blame it on me being a woman!" She shouted the last part.

Which was out of character for her. He was certain people were staring, but he didn't care. Because his sister was angry—*at him*. She'd never talked to him like this before. Never looked at him with this...disdain before. And the things she was saying...

Stomach tight, he could feel his face getting hot as he cleared his throat. "I might be a little hard on—"

"No." She tossed her unused napkin onto the table, her jaw tight. "I hadn't planned to have this conversation with you today. And definitely not in public. But I'm sick of your bullshit. I'm sick of ignoring the subtle digs only because you're my brother and you raised me. I'm grateful to you and I love working with you, but I'm done listening to your nonsense. So consider this your warning—next time you say some bullshit, I'm calling you out right then and there. And for the record, Berkley Knight is one of the nicest, funniest humans I've ever met. I know you bought into the whole 'wild Knight' version of her and have this weird obsession with her husband—"

"I'm not obsessed with her *ex*-husband," he growled. If he was being brutally honest with himself, he wasn't sure he even liked Henry Moore anymore. But he'd saved Clover's life. *Literally.* So yeah, he was grateful to the guy for the surgery he'd performed on his sister. And fine, maybe at one time he'd really liked the guy. But the last few times he'd seen him, the man had been...off. Maybe that was the right word. Or maybe he was just showing Nick who he really was. But he'd seen the guy tear into a barista as if the woman had funded a terrorist organization instead of just getting the wrong syrup type.

"Yeah, well, for your information, her ex-husband might be a talented surgeon, but he was cheating on her for years. And he hit on me during one of my check-ins. The guy is a grade A asshole with a god complex." She rolled her eyes.

Henry had cheated on Berkley? Wait... "He hit on you?"

"That's your takeaway from this?" She let out a growl of frustration then shoved her chair back. "I'm done with this conversation. I'll see you at work on Monday—and you're taking that meeting with Berkley tomorrow. I didn't tell you about it because I knew you'd balk at working with her for whatever reason you've cooked up in your mind to dislike her. So you're meeting with her, and it's going to be your first day of learning not to be an asshole!"

Oh, people were absolutely staring at them now. Unabashedly so. The entire restaurant had gone silent as Clover yelled at him.

At least no one appeared to be recording the scene. He tossed a twenty onto the table, and hurried after his sister. But by the time he made it outside she'd disappeared into one of the many shops on the main strip of Sanctuary Falls.

When his phone buzzed, he read the incoming text from Clover. *Look, I love you more than anything, but you're turning into Dad. If you don't want that, I hope you seriously reevaluate yourself and your immediate thoughts. I'm also not sorry for that explosion, though I could have chosen a more private place. I'll send you the details about tomorrow. And I'll find my own ride home. I can't see you or talk to you right now. Xo*

He wanted to deny everything she'd said but... He scrubbed a hand over his face as he made his way back to his truck. They'd parked about a mile back to enjoy downtown, so now he had plenty of time alone with his thoughts.

The last place he wanted to be.

He wasn't as bad as Clover said... Was he? They both loathed their father. He'd been an abusive, cruel man who'd broken their mother in a thousand different ways until she finally drank herself to death. Leaving them to fend for themselves against him. The little boy he'd once been hadn't understood why his mom hadn't protected them but he'd gotten over that.

Or he'd told himself that he had.

Maybe his sister was right. She'd...been a victim too. And sometimes he found himself angrier at their mother's ghost than their unfortunately still-living dad most days. A man he hadn't talked to in over a decade.

As he made it back to his truck, he thought about calling Clover, but knew it was too soon. He just knew that he didn't like this sick feeling in his gut. He and Clover never argued. About anything.

It had always been the two of them against their father, while their mother hid away, passed out in her room. He'd been the one to protect Clover against that bastard. Then when she'd come to work for him, he'd thought... Clearly she'd been bottling up a lot. And she wasn't an overreactive person.

If anything, the two of them had learned to keep their emotions locked down over the years to avoid triggering their alcoholic father, so the fact that she'd blown up at him like that, and in public... He was going to take it seriously.

And self-reflect. But later.

As he got into his truck, he forced himself not to think about his sister's words...or how stunning Berkley Knight had been. As always.

He rarely let himself look directly at her.

She was like this ray of actual sunshine, and every time he was in her vicinity, he found himself wanting to orbit around her. To get to know her better. To follow up on never calling her because of a man...he apparently shouldn't have even trusted.

Which was ridiculous. He'd never allowed himself to be close to a woman. To be vulnerable. That was how you ended up locked in a relationship, miserable and looking for a way to get out. No thanks.

But about a year ago he'd asked for her number. Then he'd let the words of someone who was apparently a cheating asshole sway him. Maybe it was because he'd *wanted* to believe them. Because the thought of getting to know her, of eventually being disappointed, had been too much.

Shoving all that bullshit down deep, he started making phone calls on his drive home. Might be Saturday, but with all the construction contracts he had going, he never stopped. And work would distract him from thinking about the accusations his sister had hurled at him.

"Hello?" a female voice said over the line.

Frowning, he glanced at his dash, saw he'd called the right number. "Ah, I'm calling for James."

There was a beat of silence, then the woman said, "This is Detective Knight. Is this Nick Storm?"

The oldest of the Knight siblings. And his name would be on the caller ID. "Yeah. What's going on?"

"What's your relationship with Mr. Reed?"

"I'm handling a contract for him." He owned a construction company, built homes all over the state. But he also did gut and reno jobs or flips if they were large enough to turn a profit. And he had a bad feeling about this.

"Would you mind coming down to the station to talk to us? I'd rather talk to you in person than over the phone."

Sighing, he took a left turn instead of heading in the direction of his home. "Yeah, I can be there in ten."

He wasn't close to James Reed, but he'd liked the guy well enough to accept a gut and reno job of four, six-condo buildings the man had recently bought up. He'd been looking forward to the job, to seeing what they could do with the condos.

If a detective was answering his phone, Nick knew that didn't mean anything good for Reed.

Chapter 5

KRYSTAL KNIGHT STEPPED THROUGH the mudroom door into her kitchen...and stared. Today had been ridiculously long.

And her three boys and husband had promised to clean up. Her birthday was tomorrow and the kitchen had a sink full of dishes, some kind of red liquidy mess smeared into it, and she bet if she opened the door under the sink... *Yep*.

Trash was overflowing.

Over the last few months it was like her family had turned into ravenous bears since she'd been promoted. There were four of them, and they hadn't been picking up any of the slack.

She could hear her oldest gaming in the next room, was pretty sure she could pinpoint where the others were based on habits.

And...she wasn't going to stay. Because if she did, she was going to lose her mind.

Grabbing her keys off the hook she'd put them on only seconds before, she headed right back out. But before she left the driveway, she texted her husband.

Stopped by the house for a minute but got called out. Can you please make sure the kitchen and bathrooms are clean before I get back? The boys were supposed to do it today and I'm tired of being the only bad guy.

She was tired of a lot of things right now, but this wasn't the moment for that particular conversation.

Of course, on it!

His reply was instant which gave her a little hope, but she still gave it only a fifty-fifty chance of anything being done.

But she shelved that thought as she drove to see Myron Booker—a bookie with the last name Booker. "Can't make this shit up," she muttered to herself.

Unlike what was normally portrayed on television, detectives actually had set hours. She should be home right now, unwinding for the day, but she just hadn't been able to face getting onto her kids and husband about the state of the house. And she wouldn't have been able to relax with the house in such a state.

So she was going to follow up on a lead she'd been planning to hit tomorrow. She texted her partner to let him know what she was doing and made the short drive to the sports bar Myron operated out of. Her partner gave her a thumbs-up and said he'd see her in the morning, but to make sure she checked in when she left.

Peter was a solid partner like that.

Ever since sports betting became legal in North Carolina only two years ago, Myron had gotten his license and was fully legit. But he'd been a bookie for a lot longer than that. *Allegedly.*

And since her dead guy had a bunch of debts, including one to Myron, she was starting with him. Especially since he had a soft spot for her and he might give her extra intel on the others Reed had owed money to.

"Hey, Bill. He in?" she asked as she passed the busy bar. She'd stripped off her Sanctuary Falls pullover in the SUV and put on her normal Columbia puffer coat to blend more.

It was already two deep on a Saturday night and she knew it could get up to three deep later. This place had been around for decades, passed on to Myron from his dad—who'd also had his hand in gray area businesses.

Bill gave her a half smile and nodded. "Yep. He'll have seen you on the cameras. Just go on back."

She knocked once, then opened the door without waiting because she was in that kind of mood.

Myron, all six foot three of him, looked up from his desk. "You're the only one who gets away with that."

She sniffed once, glanced around the beat-up office—and narrowed her gaze at the old picture of the two of them on the bookshelf. "What the hell is that?"

"Found our old prom picture, decided to frame it." He grinned, looking like the Cheshire cat.

"You're an asshole," she muttered, no heat in her voice as she basically collapsed into the seat across from him.

He frowned at her, as if really seeing her now. "You okay? Want a drink?"

"No. I mean, I do, but no. I'm still working." Technically. "What can you tell me about James Reed?"

He paused for a moment and she knew he was racking that annoyingly big brain of his. "Owns a couple run-down condos, apartment buildings and some other assets I can't think of right now. He also owes me ten large."

She knew about the condo thing from Nick Storm, so at least that lined up. "He's dead. Murdered." She didn't think Myron had killed him, but still wanted to gauge his reaction. And she'd still be looking into his alibi, but ten thousand wasn't enough for someone like Myron to kill over.

Myron's eyebrows raised slightly. "Am I a suspect?"

"He did owe you money." She kept her tone neutral.

"If I killed everyone who owed me money..." He trailed off, laughing lightly. "When was he killed? I can tell you if I have an alibi or not."

She gave him the time frame and he pulled out a piece of paper, scribbled a name and number on it.

"I was here at the bar last night until about midnight, then spent the rest of my evening, until about eight this morning, with the woman on that paper. Her place has cameras and if she hasn't deleted her Ring videos, I'm on them."

Easy enough. "Thanks... So, you know anything more about him? Any enemies, scorned lovers?"

He paused again, tapping his finger on the desk. "He's not one of my bigger clients, so off the top of my head, I don't have much. I do know that when I rejected him for another bet—because my instinct told me he wasn't a good one and apparently I was right—he went to Louis Cain, over in—"

"Wilmington. Yeah, I've heard the name." And what she knew of Cain wasn't good. The guy wasn't just a bookie, but into drugs as well. *Allegedly.*

Myron straightened slightly in his chair, the creak long and loud in the quiet office, his expression startled. "Don't go see Cain on your own. He's not like me. He's got a penchant for violence and he won't care that you're a cop."

She gave him a bemused look. "You worried about me?"

"Of course I am."

"I have no plans to talk to him alone or on his turf. I know how to do my job." She'd go with her partner, get a feel for Cain's bar and see if she could get a warrant.

He leaned back slightly, his expression losing that tightness. "I know you do... You ever think about what-if?"

She blinked. "What if, what?"

"You know, us? If I hadn't—"

"Cheated on me with Laurie Sajeski on prom night?"

"That was on prom night?" He winced.

"Wow." Krystal stood, snagged the picture of the two of them off the shelf and tucked it under her arm. "You really are an asshole and you're losing this now."

His grin was charming, part of the reason she'd fallen for him all those years ago. But she was older, wiser. And once he'd cheated on her, that had been it. She was never going to put up with that shit from anyone.

They wouldn't have lasted anyway because he was just too damn selfish, but if she was ever in real trouble, he was still on her list of people she could call for help. So there was that.

"You really never think about me?" he persisted. Because of course he did.

"No." She lifted a shoulder. "I've got a great husband and three incredible boys I can't imagine my world without, so no." Though on days like today, she had to remind herself of that. Because she loved them, but she was over this selfish teenage phase.

He sighed, placed his hand over his heart, but didn't stop her from taking the picture. "You wound me."

"Yeah, yeah. If you hear anything about Reed, let me know?"

"Of course."

Once she was back in her work vehicle, she tossed the frame in the back seat, then checked her texts and emails—anything to distract her from going home—and saw a note from their tech with James Reed's phone records. One phone number was highlighted a couple times and there was a note.

Saw the owner of this one, figured you'd want to talk to them.

When she realized who it was, she frowned. Berkley had exchanged a handful of calls with James Reed, which could mean nothing.

But she needed to talk to her sister immediately.

<h1 style="text-align:center">Chapter 6</h1>

Berkley opened her front door, surprised to find Krystal on the other side looking exhausted and serious. "Hey, got your text, what's up?" she asked even as she took a step back.

Oh god, did her sister know that she'd woken up in a dead guy's house? Had she found evidence linking her to the murder? Maybe she was here to arrest her. Berkley wondered if Krystal would let her brush her teeth before she hauled her in.

The bottom of her stomach dropped out as her sister stepped inside, stripped off her coat. "Just wanted to talk to you about something. You know a guy named James Reed?"

"No." The lie stuck in her throat. Though technically she *didn't* know him.

Her sister slipped off her boots as she held out her tablet. "These phone records say otherwise."

Berkley scanned the PDF file on the tablet. "Oh, this is Dana's phone. I mean, it's a company phone, but this is her number."

"I figured it was something like that since it wasn't your actual number. But you show up as the owner of record."

"I'm the owner of record on four different numbers." The fact that Dana, one of her part-time employees, had been talking with him could mean nothing. But it also might be important. She had no way to know. Berkley tried to keep her expression calm and normal and not let on that she'd been in the guy's house that morning.

God, had it only been that morning? Whatever, if she had to, she'd take this to the grave.

"I know," Krystal said around a yawn as she let her head roll back. "I found that out on the drive here."

"Why are you here so late? I mean, it's not late, late, but I know you get off at five or six." It was close to eight now. Well past time when Krystal usually made it home to her family. Maybe…she really did know more than she was letting on? Berkley's gut tightened again even though Krystal's body language was relaxed.

"I'm here because I didn't want to go home," her sister said bluntly.

"Why not? Also, why are you asking me about someone named James Reed?" Berkley figured that if she had no knowledge of the guy, it would be normal to wonder why Krystal was asking about him. Even though the absolute last thing she wanted to do was talk about him.

"My family is making me nuts, and Reed is connected to an ongoing investigation. Do you have anything edible here?"

Berkley snort-laughed, some of the tension in her shoulders easing as she finally led her sister into the kitchen. Their normal gathering place. "I actually do. I've got a couple burritos Silvia dropped off, courtesy of her mom."

"Her mom's an angel. How's she doing anyway? With all the health stuff."

"I'm not sure. She's been quiet about it when I ask and I haven't pushed. I think I'm going to though. I'm worried she's shouldering too much on her own."

"Probably a good idea." Krystal sighed as she sat at the island top.

Berkley slid the burritos into the oven, not waiting for it to preheat. When her sister didn't grumble about it, she knew something was definitely off. Because Krystal believed that not waiting until the preheat was at full temperature was a mortal sin. "Is everything okay with you and Mike? Or is this work stuff?"

"Mike and I are okay. The kids are just at a tough age and the transition with my new job has been a lot for everyone, that's all."

"If you're sure… Are we still on for tomorrow? Because I've got your birthday sash and crown all ready to go." She pulled out lemon sparkling water, Krystal's favorite, and poured her a glass.

"Definitely still on. No work on Sundays for me. Technically I shouldn't be working today either, but we needed to get a jump on things and one of our detectives has been out sick."

"I'm sorry it's been such a strain on you."

Krystal shrugged.

"Other than not wanting to go home, is the case the only reason you came over here today?" The oven beeped that the preheat was finally done, which meant their burritos would be done soon. And it was better this way anyway because it slowly heated up from the inside, something her sister refused to believe.

"No." Krystal slid off the stool and started pulling out sour cream and guacamole from the fridge, taking over in the way of a big sister who'd been here hundreds of times and had helped Berkley organize her kitchen when she'd moved in. "I'm just feeling weird about my thirty-fifth birthday, and you're the only person who's never made me cry on my actual birthday. I wanted to see you."

Berkley blinked as surprise shot through her for a multitude of reasons. "You wanted to see me?" Did her throat catch? Why yes it did.

Krystal frowned at her. "Of course I did, dummy. I want to see you all the time."

Berkley pulled her into a hug as a weird wave of emotion overwhelmed her. She'd gotten her life together years ago but sometimes it still bowled her over that maybe her family didn't see her as that same screw-up anymore. And she was scared that this murder would drag her back into the muck. Then she felt like shit for worrying more about herself than some dead guy. Why was being a human so complicated?

"Hey, hey." Krystal patted her back gently. "We can't both be all emotional."

She laughed against her sister's shoulder and pulled back. "Can you also explain this whole 'I'm the only one who's never made you cry on your birthday'? Because what the ever-loving hell is that about?"

"I'm not going to get into details, but yeah, my boys have all been absolute nightmares at one point or another on my birthday. And Mike forgot it three years ago."

"You said everyone though. Did...our dumbass brothers also make you cry?"

"Why do you sound gleeful?" Krystal threw a dish towel right at her face.

"Come on, I'm the family black sheep! I know I made you shed a lot of tears over the years."

"Well not on my birthday. You...have actually made all my birthdays wonderful. The balloon arches, the silly decorated cupcakes, you always go all out. In case I haven't said it enough, thank you. And please don't call yourself the black sheep. You screwed up when you were younger, sure, but you've paid for it and absolutely no one is holding it against you."

She chose to ignore the last part and preened slightly. "I'm going to make a sash for myself that says I'm the only Knight sibling to never make you cry on your birthday! I'm wearing it tomorrow."

"I can't tell if you're joking."

Berkley simply grinned as the timer went off. "Guess you'll find out tomorrow," she said as she pulled out their food. The scent of it hit her as they both groaned.

"I don't even care if you do," Krystal muttered, then frowned as she glanced at her buzzing phone.

Berkley wanted to ask if it was work or personal, but asking about her work felt too deceptive. She hated keeping anything from her sister, but Micah was right, she couldn't tell Krystal anything. It would put her in an impossible situation.

"Oh, guess who I saw today? Nick Storm," her sister said before she could answer.

Berkley made a face. "I saw him too. At Brunch and Bliss. Where'd you see him?"

"Ah, work-related."

"Oh, well I guess mine was work-related too. Ish. He was out with his sister and as charming as ever," she said dryly.

Krystal snickered. "He really does have a stick up his ass, doesn't he? A guy that good-looking shouldn't be allowed to be so insufferable. Though he wasn't too bad when I interviewed him. He was really polite."

"He knew the guy involved in your investigation?" she asked carefully, hating this line she was crossing.

"Sort of. I can't talk about it."

"I get it." And she did. So she changed the subject even though she wanted nothing more than to grill her sister to find out what the hell had really happened.

Who was James Reed? And more importantly, who had killed him?

Chapter 7

Berkley had all the windows open in the downstairs of the Queen Anne mansion. She also had on a surgical-grade mask, and it had gone a long way in combating all the dust floating around in this place. But it was still a nightmare of *stuff* everywhere and she refused to get sick on this job. She'd learned her lesson when she'd first started clearing out homes and this was one of the larger, most interesting jobs she'd agreed to take on. She couldn't wait to tell Clover what she'd found…

She turned as she heard the front door opening. She'd arrived early and had discovered that Clover tended to show up ten minutes late in general. Which was fine with her since it gave her a buffer to work with.

But it wasn't Clover who stepped into the room. It was Nick Storm. Tall, dark hair, Hollywood handsome…ugh. Too bad he was a jerk.

Her smile froze behind her mask. "Oh, it's you."

Uh oh, had she said that out loud? Yes, she definitely had.

He stopped in the entryway of the high-ceilinged kitchen, his eyes widening slightly. "Good morning," he murmured, glancing around. "I take it Clover didn't tell you I was coming?"

"Nope." But she forced herself to adapt. She could be scrupulously professional, especially for a job this big. They were supposed to sign the contract today so she quieted the voice in her head that wanted to snark at Nick just because. "Do you need a mask? It's dustier than you think."

"Ah yes, thank you." He took the one she held out and she was careful not to let her fingers touch his.

He unnerved her in more ways than one and she refused to let him get to her today. There was enough going on in her head without that nonsense swimming around up there.

She glanced at her phone as it buzzed, hid a wince. "Clover just texted." Apparently her texting style was the same as her arrival style. Late, late, *late*.

"Sounds about right," he murmured, though there was humor in his tone instead of annoyance. Which gave him a few points.

"I've already scanned all the rooms and have found a few very interesting items. I'm sure you know this already, but I told Clover I could only give a final estimate once I did a full walk-through. The final price will be almost double than what I originally—"

"Double?"

She cleared her throat at the interruption. Apparently only one of them was polite. "Correct."

His eyebrows dipped down, his lower face hidden by the mask, but his expression was clear enough. "I talked to JR King Auctions on the way here and they gave me a price based on square footage. It's less than your original quote."

Yeah, of course they had. Those guys were thieves. Something she thought Clover knew as well. Apparently she and her brother weren't on the same page. "Okay then, it sounds like your mind is already made up. Good luck working with them." She held back a snort, glad she hadn't told him about the pristine lynx fur coat she'd found in one of the upstairs bedrooms.

Though deep down, she knew she'd end up telling Clover about it before JR King Auctions swept in. Only because she liked the other woman.

"Wait, I didn't say I wanted to work with them."

"Didn't you?"

"I just said that they came in with a lower offer. I'm sure you can match them."

She snorted softly, desperate to get out of this kitchen and house altogether. The room was stacked full of boxes, and even though it was the least crowded in the entire house, she was still far too close to Nick—who somehow smelled amazing even in the midst of the musty scent lingering. She still hated that she'd actually given him her number once upon a time.

He'd been the first man she'd considered dating since her divorce, at that. She'd been so stunned and awkward that she hadn't been sure if she should even say yes. Then he'd never called, so it hadn't mattered. And anytime after that when she'd run into him, he'd been weirdly cold to her.

"I don't do business like that. I charge based on how full the house is. It would be insane to charge based on square footage. And for the record, your sister already knew that. I'm not sure what you guys are trying to pull—"

"Clover doesn't know I called them." He held up his palms. "I just made a few calls this morning to double-check your number."

"Well if you're not going to go with me, I still hope you don't go with JR King Auctions. I'm not telling you this for any reason other than I really like your sister. Go with the Johnson Brothers. They're solid and won't rob you blind." She picked up her purse and was surprised when he followed her outside.

Tugging off the mask, she inhaled the crisp morning air as they descended the stairs.

"Look, I didn't mean to offend you."

She couldn't hide a snort. "I'm pretty sure you don't care if you offend me."

His eyes widened slightly, but other than that she couldn't read his expression. He cleared his throat. "Clover really wants to do business with you."

Yeah, well, Clover wasn't there, and just looking at this man had all her hackles rising. God, why did he have to be so annoyingly handsome? It was a crime, simple as that. "It's pretty clear you need to get on the same page as your sister. I was under the impression that we would be signing the contract today, but clearly that's not the case. Do your due diligence, call around, and figure things out. If you two decide you still want to go into business, maybe we can talk." She took a deep breath, calling on all her patience. "And if you do decide to go with JR King Auctions, don't let them in that house unsupervised. They will absolutely steal from you."

She could tell he wanted to argue with her, but he nodded. "I'll talk to my sister about this."

"Sounds like a good plan. And..." God, she should just keep her mouth shut. "There's a lynx coat in there that's been preserved and worth at least a hundred and seventy-five thousand dollars—but I think you can get more for it." And she would have gotten a nice commission on the sale had they chosen to sell it. "I put it in the pantry and had planned to show Clover as a surprise." She'd also found a few other really cool items—like a vintage uranium glass vase—but the fur was the big-ticket piece.

"Are you serious?"

"Yep. Talk to you later." Or never. She got into her Bronco and left, glad he hadn't blocked her in.

She tried not to let the disappointment get to her, but this had been the job of a lifetime. A historic mansion absolutely packed with untold goodies just waiting to be discovered. She'd barely even scratched the surface of what was inside. And anything they sold within the first two years that she'd valued for them over a certain price, she'd have gotten a sweet commission. That clause was just in there for people who wanted to be sneaky and hold on to things until they could sell on their own. The majority of people just wanted their homes cleaned out, everything put up for auction, and to be done with it.

Nick and Clover had bought this mansion with the intent to clean it out, update a few things, make a profit from the auction, then sell the mansion once it was staged and make an even bigger profit. It was a huge investment for them—one with incredible return potential—and she'd been so looking forward to adding this to her portfolio.

She was a little mad at herself for telling him about the coat, but...whatever. Just because he was a jerk didn't mean she had to be one too.

When she saw the time, she decided to head to Krystal's place. She was early but she could grab lattes for the both of them and spend an extra hour before the party madness started. She was kind of surprised that Mike hadn't texted asking her or the others to bring anything to the party but figured he must have it under control.

She'd brought some extra balloons, a party sash and crown, as well as her present as backup just in case the place wasn't as blinged-out as it should be.

Because her big sister deserved the best.

***

"Hey Aunt B." Jett, still wearing pajama pants and no T-shirt, hugged her as she stepped into the foyer. "What are you doing here?"

Berkley laughed lightly as she hugged him, realized he definitely needed a shower. Or deodorant. God, when had he grown into this young man? "Ha ha. Where's your mom?"

"Ah, kitchen I think, but I'm not sure." His twin brothers shouted for him from somewhere in the house and he ran off before she could even shut the front door.

"Teenagers," she muttered, still not sure how her sister and Mike had handled Jett, Miles and River when they were younger. Hell, she wasn't sure how they handled them now that they were thirteen-year-old twins and fourteen.

Because that was a lot of stinky teenage boys in one house. She shuddered, not in a rush to have kids any time soon. Not that she didn't adore her nephews, but taking care of another human was a lot.

As she stepped into the kitchen she found Krystal sitting at the island top, drinking coffee.

"Hey, happy birthday." She set the extra latte in front of her, then pulled the birthday crown out of her bag of tricks, ready to set it on Kyrstal's head, but frowned when she saw the expression on her sister's face. "What..." She glanced around the kitchen, realized it was sort of a disaster.

And there were no decorations anywhere.

And her sister was dressed adorably in an off the shoulder sparkly cream sweater, her makeup done in a way she normally only did for nights out on the town... *Oh my god.*

Noooo.

"Do me a favor and go get in my car?" She pulled out her keys, tossed them to Krystal who of course caught them with her panther-like reflexes.

"It's fine." Krystal looked close to crying though, her green eyes watery.

Oooh, noooo.

"It's fine that they forgot your birthday?" Berkley asked it as a question because she wasn't a hundred percent sure.

Swallowing hard, Krystal picked up the latte, her hands trembling slightly.

"My car. Now. It's your birthday so you have to listen to me."

"That's not how that works but...fine." Krystal, just looking like someone had kicked a puppy, left with the keys in hand.

"Grab your coat on the way out," Berkley called out because they were going to be gone for a while.

Berkley waited until she heard the front door shut, then went in search of Mike, who was on his computer, working on something. She knew he had a big job he'd been working on with his new company, but come on. This was one day. Hell, it was just a few hours. "Mike, hey."

He turned, clearly surprised to see her. "Hey. Ah, morning. Krystal's in the kitchen I think."

"Oh I know. I need to see you in the living room. It's important." She turned on her heel before he could respond. Then she stalked into the living room and unplugged the television—while her nephews were gaming.

"Hey!"

"What the hell!"

"Why'd you do that, Aunt B?"

She held up her hand, ignoring them as Mike walked in. "All of you sit down right now." To her surprise, they actually did, watching her curiously. And a little cautiously.

Probably because she looked rabid—if her face matched her inner rage, it was a good possibility.

"What's today, you guys?" she asked as she clapped her hands together once.

"Ah...Sunday?" Jett asked hopefully.

God, she loved that kid even as she wanted to shake all of them. "Sure is. What else is today?"

Mike, looking annoyed at her, cleared his throat. "Look, Berkley, if you could just tell us—"

"Tell you that you missed your wife's birthday? That the whole family will be over in an hour for a party you're clearly not ready for."

Mike's eyes widened as he pulled his phone out, likely to double-check his calendar.

"Oh, I'm not wrong," she gritted out, the tether on her anger about to break free.

"Why didn't you—"

"I know you're not going to ask why I didn't remind you," she snapped in a voice she'd never used with any of them before. "This woman loves you more than anything—pushed your big-ass heads out of her body and would literally die for you. And she makes a huge deal out of all your birthdays—I know, I've been to *all* the parties."

All four of them stared at her with expressions of horror, hopefully at themselves. "Your mom—and your wife—is in my car right now. I'm taking her out for a birthday brunch." Or lunch at this point. "By the time I get back, this place better be sparkling and full of fucking cheer."

The boys' eyes widened.

"Don't act shocked. I know you hear worse on TV and at school." Okay maybe not, but whatever, she was barely hanging on to her temper.

Mike shot to his feet. "Jesus, I can't believe—"

"Oh no. You're not going to apologize to her with words now. And honestly I don't know that you're going to fix this at all today. I'm not married, but even I know this sucks big-time." The kids got a break because they were teenagers. They could barely remember to brush their teeth some days. But Mike... "And I'd just like to remind you that Krystal is smart as hell and so gorgeous that she can pull any..." She'd been about to say *dick* but held back at the last moment when she realized the boys were still staring at her. "Guy she wants. Literally everywhere we go, she gets hit on."

"Ew!" Jett made a barfing sound.

"Sorry guys, your mom is hot and impressive, though that's not the important thing." She was focusing all her attention on Mike, who was looking panicked and shell-shocked at the same time. "The important thing is you don't lose sight of the big picture of your life. Of the person I know you love more than anything."

And on that note, she stormed out properly even as she group texted all her siblings except Krystal. *Get over to Krystal's house ASAP! The family forgot her birthday and the house is a disaster. I'm taking her out for a couple hours but I've never seen her look so defeated.*

She received a barrage of texts from the other three all saying they'd be there within ten minutes. And Apollo made a couple threats against Mike, which, despite how much she normally adored Krystal's husband, made Berkley snicker.

She also saw that she had three missed calls from Nick Storm and one from his sister. She ignored them as she slid into the front seat and tore out of the driveway.

She wasn't sure what was wrong with her sister's husband, but she refused to let Krystal's day be ruined.

Chapter 8

"I know I shouldn't say this, but I love drunk Krystal. I mean, I love you all the time, but this is fun." It was freezing out, but Berkley had grabbed an old family quilt, a couple bottles of prosecco and a bunch of mini desserts and cheeses from the grocery store. Now, two hours later, they were sitting at a deserted park on the merry-go-round stuffing their faces.

"I'm not drunk." Krystal sniffed once before she downed her prosecco. Then she picked up a petit four and popped it whole in her mouth. "Just tipsy."

"It's sexy when you talk with your food showing."

Krystal rolled her eyes, but laughed. "Whatever. I'm not even mad anymore. Just..." She let out a short scream. "Look, I get it. Mike is busy with his new job. I'm busy too, and I thought we were partners. Part of me thinks..."

Berkley straightened. "Is he cheating on you?"

"What! No. Oh my god, I don't think so. That would never even..." She trailed off, frowning as she took another sip of her bubbly.

"No, of course he's not. You just paused so I panicked. Mike would never cheat. He loves you too much." Berkley's ex had cheated and she'd been pretty blind to it—in the beginning. It was impossible to imagine solid, stoic Mike cheating though. Or Krystal not picking up on it. "How many times has he texted you?"

"Seventeen last I looked." Her tone was dry. "I think he's given up."

"Micah sent me some pictures of the house. Everything looks good if you want to head home and see everyone." She couldn't get a read on her sister though.

"I'd like to run away, but since that's not an option..." She stood, wavered on her feet once, then straightened. "Are you good to drive?"

"I had one glass two hours ago. I'm more than good. Though you better save some of that gouda for me."

"My birthday, I'll eat it all." She popped another cheese cube in her mouth before she started to help clean everything up.

But Berkley shooed her away. "I've got this. Just chill. This is your day and you're not doing anything else."

Her phone buzzed again, the insistent sound getting on her last nerve.

"Oh my god, who keeps texting you?" Krystal asked as they trekked back to her car.

"Oh...I don't know. Probably Nick Storm," she said, wincing a little.

"Why...oh. The job with Clover. What happened with that? I thought you were meeting up with her...oh, today."

"Yeah, earlier this morning. I'm not sure it's going to work out. And we don't need to talk about it now anyway." She didn't want to burden Krystal with all the details, not when she had enough on her plate.

"I'd rather talk about that than complain about myself anymore. Please, distract me."

"Fine." She filled her sister in on how that morning had gone on the short drive back to Krystal's house—which had ridiculously huge balloons outside, spelling out *happy birthday*.

Inside was more of the same. It was probably over-the-top—as it should be—but her boys were being so sweet and Krystal was actually laughing, so bring it on. Krystal was much more forgiving than Berkley would have been. Or maybe she was just covering up her hurt and burying it down deep. Because that's what Berkley liked to do with her own feelings. Suuuuper healthy.

"You look a little murdery," Berkley murmured to her brother Apollo as she approached him next to the food buffet on the island.

He was angrily popping meatballs onto his plate. "Probably because I'm contemplating making Krystal a widow."

"It's fine, they're going to work it out. Besides, you've all made her cry on her birthday before. Except me." Berkley knew that if she didn't keep Apollo distracted, he was likely to go off on Mike.

Which would just ruin everything.

"Wait, what?" He stared at her as if she'd lost her mind.

She smirked. "Yep. Every single one of you has made her cry on her birthday at some point," she whispered, realizing she probably shouldn't feel smug, but also not caring.

Because her siblings all had their shit together and this was the *one* thing she'd done better than them.

Damn, my bar is really low. Pathetic. She shook her head. *Whatever.*

"You're full of shit."

She shrugged. "I mean, sometimes, but not with this."

Apollo eyed her, then nodded at Micah. "You hear this?"

She steered them out onto the back patio where there were more decorations and a little dessert tower, to be joined by their brother Cormac as well. Cormac shoved a mini pink velvet cupcake in his mouth as she crowed about her victory of not making Krystal cry.

"You look so smug," Apollo muttered as he finally accepted that she was right.

"You're just lucky I'm not wearing my sash saying so. I didn't want to make the boys feel bad," she added. "But I have one, and next get-together, I'm wearing it. Might even make myself a matching crown."

Her three brothers stared at her.

Cormac was the first to blink. "There's something wrong with you."

"There's something wrong with *all* of us." She patted his arm and headed back inside because she wanted some of those meatballs, and to check on her sister.

Luckily things were normal enough and everyone seemed to enjoy themselves for the next couple hours.

Though she had no doubt that Krystal and Mike needed to talk things out. Because the smile Krystal was putting on for Mike, oh that was super fake. Maybe she wasn't burying her emotions the same way Berkley did. Hell, hopefully she wasn't.

***

"Is everything really okay with them?" Micah asked Berkley as he walked her out to her car later. "I can't believe Mike actually forgot her birthday."

"They're fine." She had no idea if they actually were, but wasn't going to say otherwise. "He dropped the ball because of his new job." Again, she had no idea, but now wasn't the time to speculate.

"Okay good." He shoved out a sigh. "So..."

"You found something?" She glanced at the front porch, was very aware of the doorbell camera.

In response he got into her passenger seat, so she slid in behind the wheel and started the heater going full blast.

"I'm still digging through his files, but I can tell you that Reed had a lot of gambling debts. He was about to go into business with Storm Construction. A gut and reno job on a few condo buildings, from the contract I found."

That lined up with what Krystal had said about talking to Nick Storm about the dead guy. The dead guy she was trying not to obsess over, or think of by name.

"How was he going to pay for the renovations?" Because that kind of job wasn't cheap.

"That's the thing. In the last week before he died, he paid off his car and then made a couple-thousand-dollar deposits into his business account. Nothing huge to draw flags, but I can't figure out where the money came from."

"Does he have… Oh my god, like a bookie? We could talk to Myron." Krystal's long-ago ex who was sort of a jerk, but weirdly charming.

Micah gave her a dry look. "If either of us talks to him, you know he'll tell Krystal."

"Damn it, yeah." The guy might be shady as hell, but he would definitely tell their sister if they stopped by to ask about a dead guy she was investigating. So that was off the table.

"And you don't need to be worrying about this," Micah added.

"Are you kidding me? It's *all* I've been doing." The knowledge that she'd woken up in a dead guy's house with no clue how she'd gotten there was like this constant buzz at the back of her skull. It never shut off. She alternated between thinking of that and…thinking about Nick Storm and his stupid, handsome face. *Gah!* She really had to get over it. It wasn't like they'd ever shared anything anyway.

Except that morning at the coffee shop had been so…fun. And she'd allowed herself to be vulnerable, to hope for something better than her past. Maybe that was what was hanging her up so bad about him. She'd allowed herself to feel hope. Man, she really did need to get over him.

"I get that, but you can't go investigating this because Krystal will find out. I swear I'm on top of it. I've got some feelers out to see who else this guy was in debt to. And Krystal and her partner are on the job. It wasn't you, so they'll figure out who killed him."

"I guess." Or more like she hoped.

"No, no guessing. You have to live your life like normal."

"I am." Even if it felt weird. It wasn't like she'd even known the guy, but still. "But there's still someone out there who dumped me at his place. Unless it was him, but that makes no sense since he was murdered."

"I know." Micah's expression was grim. "I'm trying to figure that out too. You're being careful everywhere you go, right?"

She sniffed indignantly. "Of course." Technically she hadn't been paying attention to anything today because she'd been so worried about Krystal, but she kept that to herself.

He watched her for a long moment, then nodded. "Okay. I've got my phone on me. Call me if you feel tempted to do something stupid."

She just rolled her eyes, but nodded as he got out. And then instead of heading home, she surprised herself by calling Nick.

Not because she wanted to talk to him—a lie she told herself. Fine, whatever, she liked the sound of his voice. Even if she wanted to simultaneously punch and kiss him at the same time. She bet he'd be a good kisser, all intense and eager. Or maybe she was just projecting.

"Berkley." He answered on the first ring, sounding slightly out of breath.

And she hated that she wondered what he'd been up to. She didn't need to think about him at all. "Hey. Just returning your call." There, she sounded polite and professional. And maybe a little disinterested.

"I know it's Sunday, but would you have a few minutes to meet up? Ah, I'm at the office but I was heading out to grab a bite at Pasta Paradise... Dinner will be on me."

She paused because she loved that place—who wouldn't love a place called *Pasta Paradise*—and even if the thought of having dinner with him rattled her for more than one reason, she wanted to hear what he had to say. Because he wouldn't be asking her out to talk unless he and Clover had discussed the job.

And she was weak—she desperately wanted the chance to go through the Queen Anne mansion—aka the Carmine Mansion. It was historical and the kind of thing she'd been dreaming of since she started her business. Bessie Carmine, a famous jazz singer, had bought it in the fifties, and had been collecting things of interest for the last seventy years. Rumor had it that the original owner had been a bootlegger in the thirties, then it passed hands a few times before Bessie snapped it up and held on to it. When she'd died, he and Clover had managed to buy it quietly before it even went on the market.

But Berkley couldn't let him know how much she wanted it, so she had to sound casual. "Ah, okay, I guess I could. I'm about fifteen minutes from there. Will that give you enough time to be there?" She was going to stuff her face on his dime and just maybe salvage this contract.

"Yep. I'll see you then."

She hated the little flip in her stomach at his words. This was business, pure and simple. Nothing more. So what if she found him *mildly* attractive? God, she couldn't even lie to herself with a straight face.

But she was a professional.

And maybe if she repeated it enough, she'd start to believe herself.

Chapter 9

IT DIDN'T MATTER THAT he'd tried to prepare himself to see her, because Nick was still stunned speechless for just a moment when Berkley walked into the restaurant.

He'd chosen this place specifically—he knew it was her favorite.

And she looked good enough to eat. As always. Not that he should be thinking about her in anything other than a professional manner. He just hoped she agreed to work with him.

And not just because his sister was going to be pissed at him if he couldn't salvage this.

He wanted to spend time with Berkley. Get to know her more. Had wanted that from the moment he'd met her.

But her smile was neutral, nothing like that first genuine one he'd been hit with a year ago—and never recovered from. "Hopefully you haven't been here long," she murmured.

He stood, waiting for her to sit, and shook his head. "Just got here. Thank you for meeting with me tonight."

"It's fine. I was just leaving a birthday party, so it was good timing."

Her dark hair was down in soft waves and her green eyes held him captivated—as always. In a dark green sweater dress, shimmery tights and heeled boots, she could have been coming from a date. Something he didn't want to think about.

"Before we start, I want to apologize…" He paused as their server stepped up and took her drink order, flirting a little too heavily for his liking.

Not that it should matter, but he didn't have to like it. Still, the server didn't know this wasn't a date.

"So… You wanted to apologize?" There was a hint of mischief in her dark green eyes as she watched him across her sparkling water.

He cleared his throat. "Yes. To be blunt, I was a dick this morning."

Her eyebrows raised a fraction. "Did your sister tell you to say that?"

He snort-laughed at her bluntness. "No. I realized this all on my own. I…wasn't trying… Okay, I *was* price shopping. But that's not personal. And it has nothing to do with you. My sister has recently pointed out that I need to let her do her damn job and I should have. She'd already researched your business and you were correct in assuming that it was a done deal." He paused, trying to gauge her expression. "We would still like to sign that contract if you're open to it."

She cleared her throat, still watching him warily. Which, fine, fair. "The price might have gone up a little."

Also fair enough. "You can just call it the asshole fee for my behavior."

She let out a startled laugh and he drank in the sound. Full-bodied and so genuine, it infused him straight to his bones. "I mean, I wasn't going to say that out loud," she said, still laughing lightly. "Even if I was thinking it."

"Look, it's clear we got off on the wrong foot."

"We?" Her expression sobered.

"Fine. Me. I very clearly let my relationship with your ex-husband color my view of you, and for that I apologize."

She looked surprised, probably because he was being so blunt, then she snorted softly.

"What?" he asked.

She sighed, lifted a shoulder. "He screwed half the nurses at the hospital, yet you judged me as the bad guy in the relationship. It's frustrating because you're not the only one..." She shook her head. "Never mind, that's not professional to talk about."

"He really cheated on you?" When Clover had told him that, he'd been curious about the details. Also, what kind of moron would cheat on someone like Berkley? He hated cheating regardless, but Henry had to be the worst kind of stupid to look for someone else.

She gave him a look that said exactly how much she thought of his question. "Uh, yeah."

Okay, so his sister had been right. *Clearly* he didn't know Henry Moore at all. And at this point, he realized he had a huge blind spot and needed to pull his head out of his ass.

"But I definitely don't want to talk about him. I would, however, love to talk about the Carmine Mansion."

He smiled at the enthusiasm in her voice. "I knew you wanted the job."

"Of course I want it. But I know my worth." She said it almost defiantly, as if daring him to contradict her.

"And I respect that... Is JR King Auctions really thieves?"

"Oh yeah. They're the worst." She shuddered slightly. "They've scammed more people than I want to think about. One day they're going to mess with the wrong person and hopefully get sued. Or just get their asses kicked."

He liked how blunt she was about things, how she didn't hold back with her honesty. And yeah, he realized how very wrong he'd been about her. His first instinct when meeting her had been spot-on. She was the real deal, a genuine person who made his heart race out of control simply by being in her presence.

They spent the rest of dinner talking, partially about the contract, but a little about her family and his sister. Just surface stuff, but she'd definitely thawed on him.

He wasn't certain he deserved it, but he'd take it. Because his sister had been right. As always. She'd reamed him out again today and he'd realized that he might lose her not only as a partner if he didn't start treating her like they were equals, but in subtler ways too. Because all the shit she'd tossed at him yesterday morning had hit its mark. Even if he didn't want to dwell on it—he needed to acknowledge it. And do something about it.

"Oh, my sister said she saw you," Berkley said as the server dropped off her dessert, a chocolate ricotta cake. She got a little powdered sugar on her bottom lip and he had the sudden urge to reach out and swipe it with his thumb.

Or his tongue.

Hell. He tightened his jaw, forcing his expression to relax. He wanted her more than was sane. More than he'd ever expected to fall for someone. "Ah, yeah. For a case she's working."

"Oh."

She didn't ask more, but he didn't want a lapse in conversation so he opened up more than he normally would have. "This guy that I was about to do business with... He was killed. Ah, murdered. I don't really know the details, but I called him while your sister was at his place, I guess. So she asked me down to talk about what I knew of him."

"Oh my gosh, that's awful."

"Yeah. I honestly didn't know the guy well. Not that I'm downplaying his death, but I'd only met him a couple times."

She nodded and looked as if she wanted to say more, but then frowned as she looked past him.

He followed her gaze, saw her friend Silvia passing by the open doorway from the courtyard. The dark-haired woman glanced over at them and looked almost...panicked. Or maybe just surprised.

Silvia hurried over to them, her smile strained as she looked between both of them—frowning at him in confusion. "Hey, Berkley. Surprised to see you here."

"Oh, right. Ah, Silvia this is Nick Storm. My new..."

"Client." He held out a hand for Silvia, who was clearly dressed for a date in a body-hugging caramel-colored leather skirt, black undershirt and spiked heels. He had a sister, he knew what a 'date look' consisted of.

Silvia gave him a polite enough smile and returned his handshake before giving Berkley a hug. "I'm here on a date. I'll fill you in later," she whispered before hurrying away.

Once her friend headed back through the door that led to the seating area in the courtyard, the easy camaraderie that had wrapped around them earlier during the meal was gone and the polite professional with clear walls was back in place.

Not that he blamed her. He'd been icy toward her for the last year anytime he'd seen her and it had been based on shitty information.

Info he'd had no reason to distrust... Though considering the source, maybe he needed to run his head through a brick wall.

"Clover's taking up a couple new challenges at work so I'll be taking point on this contract." He'd apologize to his sister later for making this decision without telling her, but he needed to make things right with Berkley.

And the only way to do that was to work with her. Fine, he wanted to spend more time with her. Clover would understand. Probably.

"I'm surprised you have time." There was no rancor in her tone, just honesty.

He lifted a shoulder because she wasn't wrong. This job wasn't something he would normally oversee. "Technically this is out of my normal scope, but I love historical homes."

"Almost sounds like a confession," she whispered conspiratorially.

He grinned, surprised by how at ease he was with her. "My company makes money in modern construction and I make no apologies. People need places to live and we build quality homes that will stand the test of time... But I have a soft spot for historical renovations."

"Me too. And since you've apologized, I can admit that I'm obsessed with the Carmine Mansion. I did some research on the previous owner, and Bessie Carmine had an amazing reputation."

"Did you read the rumors of how she was suspected of burying lovers in the backyard? One theory is that she paid the owner of the company who installed the pool to bury bodies underneath it."

Her eyes widened slightly. "You researched too?"

"Her reputation is part of the reason I bought the place. I'd seen some old pictures online from the parties she used to have and the contents alone are worth preserving—and hopefully we'll make a profit on the eventual auction. I just couldn't stand the thought of someone coming in and bulldozing it without thoroughly cataloguing things. Don't get me wrong, I want to make money, but... I just couldn't let this opportunity go. And thank you for the information about that fur coat."

She shrugged, but gave him a half smile that sent a punch of heat to his gut.

As they talked about the history of the home, he lost track of time until their server stood by their table, pointedly, and cleared his throat. "We're going to be closing soon, so if you'd like to pay your tab—"

"Oh my god." Berkley glanced at her cell phone, clearly as surprised as he was by the time. "I can't believe how late it is."

He slipped his card to the man, who practically sprinted away before he'd even pulled his hand back.

"I feel so bad," Berkley whispered.

"I'll leave a bigger tip than I was planning to."

"I'm normally in my pajamas by this time... And as I'm saying that out loud, I realize how pathetic that sounds." But she was grinning.

He laughed at her dry tone. "Then we're both pathetic because I am too." And he wondered what her definition of pajamas was. Probably a lot more decent than what he was picturing—or fantasizing about.

Which he had to stop doing, he reminded himself. They were going to be working together.

By the time he'd paid, the restaurant had turned off half the lights and he heard the distinctive click of the front door lock as they stepped out onto the front patio.

She snickered as he held out her coat for her to slip on. "They certainly weren't subtle."

He shook his head and fell in step with her, earning a surprised look. "What?" he asked.

"What are you doing?"

"Ah, walking you to your car."

Her frown deepened. "You don't need to."

He scanned the dark, nearly deserted parking lot, then back at her. "And yet I'm going to."

She bristled slightly, but then looked around as if seeing their surroundings for the first time. "Fine."

So maybe they were back to strictly business. He knew he wasn't going to win her over after *one* dinner, but he thought he'd made progress.

When they neared her car, he hung back so he wouldn't crowd her. "I'll email you the contract tonight. Just redline anything you want to change."

"Sounds good. And thanks again for dinner." She slid into her vehicle and didn't waste time shutting and locking her car door.

He waited until she was out of the parking lot before getting into his own truck. As he did, an SUV he hadn't even realized was in the parking lot started up and steered out in the same direction as her.

And that was why he'd walked her to her car. The lights in this lot were bullshit. It was probably just a worker from the restaurant leaving since they were closing, but even so. No way he was letting her or any woman walk to their vehicle alone, in the dark.

Chapter 10

BERKLEY OPENED HER EYES, groaned slightly as she sat up. And almost had a panic attack.

She looked around the laundry room she was lying in—had been dumped in? What the hell was going on... *Oh no. No, no, no...* It was happening again. And she knew this laundry room well, unfortunately.

It was her ex-husband's. A set of his scrubs hung from the bar over the washing machine and dryer, a few empty hangers next to it.

As she struggled to her feet, she touched the side of her neck, winced. Had someone done something to her? Drugged her?

Through a haze, she took stock of herself. In her pajamas from last night.

And she remembered getting home after her business dinner with Nick Storm.

She'd showered, washed her face, gotten into her pajamas and then fallen asleep watching one of her comfort shows. A comedy about a chaotic family in the Midwest.

And yet here she was, with no memory of how she'd gotten here.

She looked around the room, didn't see her phone anywhere. She didn't even have shoes on.

Clearly someone was screwing with her. Trying to set her up.

And the why didn't even matter at this point.

Even as terror congealed in her gut, she forced herself to think. First she slipped on an oversized pair of sneakers, then eased open the door that led to Henry's living room.

Inside, his home was quiet. He hadn't changed much since they'd split up, no surprise. He'd barely let her make any changes when she'd moved in and had always made it clear that it was "his place." Ugh, whatever, she needed to find him. Because if someone really had dumped her here with the same intentions as at Reed's place...

She was tempted to call out, but a little voice stopped her. She didn't want to believe that Henry was behind this, but just in case, she stayed quiet.

She floated through the house on quiet feet, glad his shoes didn't squeak. At his bedroom door, she paused, then steeled herself as she nudged the partially open door fully open with her foot.

The hinge made the faintest creaking, the sound overpronounced in the unnaturally quiet house. She could see a lump under the fluffy cream-colored covers, went to step inside, but froze.

Sirens sounded in the distance. Faint, but getting closer.

Oh god, it really *was* happening again. She couldn't see if Henry was in the bed and couldn't risk checking. Even so, her instinct told her that someone had murdered him. And maybe they wanted it to look like she'd done it. Why else would she be here?

A sob caught in her throat, but now wasn't the time to panic or freak out. She had to act. To move.

To get the hell out of here!

She raced back to the laundry room. As adrenaline surged through her, she grabbed a dark hoodie from the laundry basket and slipped it on. She pulled the hood over her head and tightened the string around her face. Then she snagged Henry's gloves tossed on top of the shoe rack. Gloves she'd bought him almost four years ago. They'd been divorced for two years, she was surprised he still had them. Not that it mattered now.

She had to get out of here.

Before the cops arrived.

Or anyone saw her.

She knew she was going to have to tell her sister everything, but she couldn't do it this way. Couldn't get charged by the cops for something she hadn't done. Because then she'd be locked up and they'd have already made their decision about her. And a jury would absolutely convict her. She would be painted as a jealous or spurned ex-wife. The man was a god around here so there was no way she'd get a fair trial.

She knew how the world worked. People in this town judged her simply for having the audacity to divorce Henry.

And maybe she was wrong. Maybe...he wasn't really dead and there was another explanation for her being here. Maybe the person in his bed had only been sleeping.

Keeping her head down, she slipped out of the laundry room into the attached garage. Her heart rate jacked up as the alarm went off.

Wait, so she'd been in his house *with* the alarm set?

What. The. Hell.

Unable to hear the police siren anymore over the noise, she hurried out the side door into his backyard.

Since she knew where his cameras were, she kept her head angled down and jumped the fence. Her heart was in her throat as she raced across the neighbor's backyard, the constant *thud, thud, thud* a staccato tattoo telling her to run like hell.

And never look back.

The sun wasn't up yet, but it had to be close given the way the sky was lightening into faint oranges and purples. Which meant there would be people out soon.

Knowing that she had to get somewhere safe—to hide—before someone saw her running around in pajamas, she headed to the closest place she knew of.

Twenty minutes later, Micah opened his front door for her, frowning as he took in her attire. And the fear on her face as she gasped for breath.

"I woke up in Henry's place. In his laundry room," she blurted. "Someone must have drugged me at home and dragged me there." She touched the side of her neck as she spoke.

Tugging her inside, he shut the door behind her and leaned down to inspect her neck. "Someone stuck you with something." He looked absolutely murderous.

She froze at a sound somewhere in the back of his house, but he waved it off.

"It's fine. I've got someone over."

"Oh." She shook herself, not caring at the moment.

"Tell me everything."

She quickly recapped how she'd woken up in the laundry room, saw what looked like a body in Henry's bed, then raced over here. Then said, "We need to tell Krystal."

Micah was silent for a long moment, but slowly nodded. "Fine, but it'll be on your terms. Change out of these clothes. I'm holding on to all of them—and I'll burn them if necessary. I've got clothes you can wear and then we're going to get your blood tested."

"How—"

"I've got a friend who owes me a bunch of favors. You need your blood tested now while we can still detect...whatever might be in your system."

Moving on autopilot, she followed him into his guest room and changed into the clothes he left behind. She couldn't imagine who had done this to her, was trying to set her up for not one, but two murders. None of this made any sense, but she forced her mind to calm because she was starting to spiral.

When she came out, they headed straight to the local hospital. She was surprised when a nurse she recognized met them in one of the quieter lobbies.

The man simply nodded at Micah, then motioned for them to follow him deeper into the hospital.

She let the two of them talk to each other as the man drew her blood with surprising ease. His bedside manner was incredibly gentle, and for that she was grateful.

So much so that stupid tears started leaking out of her eyes as he put a Band-Aid on her arm.

"It's going to be okay," he murmured, holding her hand gently. "If you need more testing than this...we can ensure privacy. And a female nurse."

She blinked away the tears when she realized what he thought. "No. I don't..." She cleared her throat. "That's not why I'm crying. I'm just grateful you're being so kind."

He patted her hand again. "I'll get this worked up off the books and we'll figure out what's going on."

Her brother had told him that they suspected she'd been drugged, but not any other details. So of course he assumed she'd been assaulted. Or potentially so anyway. If she didn't still have her tampon in, she'd have assumed the same thing.

Her brother stepped out into the hallway with him, and even though she tried to eavesdrop, all she could hear was murmuring.

When Micah came back in, she stood. "I'm ready to leave." She needed to talk to Krystal, even if she was dreading it.

She might not want to deal with the cops, but she trusted her sister.

Micah nodded. "Fine, but we're going to your place first. You're showering and changing into something comfortable. And I'm contacting a lawyer. You're going to voluntarily go to the police station to talk to Krystal—with your lawyer present. And don't argue," he snapped when she went to open her mouth.

"I'm not. I just wanted to say thank you." She rushed at him for a hug, taking him off guard as he stumbled back.

He made an oomph sound, but held her tight. "We're going to figure this out, I promise."

"And you're going to tell me who was at your place this morning," she murmured into his chest, mostly because she needed to talk about anything other than what was happening.

He let out a startled laugh and stepped back. "Seriously? Now?"

"Come on, I need something to distract me," she said as they headed back to the parking garage.

"Yeah well it's not going to be with this."

"Oooh, so this is maybe serious?" And she had a feeling she knew exactly who'd been at his place. Her brother might have an incredible poker face most of the time, but he let it slip on occasion.

"This is none of your business."

"Fine." She sighed as another wave of emotion swept over her. "I still can't believe this is happening," she whispered as he drove them back to her place.

"I know. And we're going to get to the bottom of this. You've got cameras and a security system—"

"I know I set it last night!" She did it without thought every evening as part of her nightly ritual. "And if I had my damn phone, I could check the log to make sure."

"Your phone is at your place. I checked the location sharing app on mine."

Oh, right.

"You're going to need to take off your location sharing from anyone who's not family—and probably Krystal for right now."

"I can't do that." It would hurt their sister, who'd done nothing but look out for all of them since they were kids.

"You have to. And you're going to be changing your security system PIN and any password I can think of that's necessary. You're too free with that shit."

He wasn't wrong. Her friends, her cleaning service, and a few others off the top of her head all had her security code. She was busy with work and sometimes people needed to drop stuff off so...she gave them a temporary passcode. And then never deleted it from her dashboard.

"You're not even arguing?"

"Don't be smug," she muttered.

Then the bottom fell out of her world as he pulled down her street to see two patrol cars sitting in her driveway, lights flashing.

"Oh my god," she breathed out.

"Duck," Micah ordered.

Without pause, she slumped in her seat as he kept driving. "Oh my god, oh my god. Was Krystal there?"

"Yep. And she definitely saw me. But she's not following us."

"Okay, let's head to the station now and show up before I'm arrested. I'll call a lawyer. I know a couple from some jobs." And they were so damn expensive, but right about now wasn't the time to be frugal. Not when her freedom was in jeopardy.

"I've got someone in mind," her brother said.

"Someone who owes you a favor?"

"Sort of." His tone was grim, and she wasn't sure how to take it, but she trusted him.

"I know some good lawyers. You don't have to do this."

"I'm going to pretend you didn't say that."

"Fair enough," she murmured, leaning back against the headrest as the weight of everything settled on her.

When Krystal's name flashed on the dash of Micah's SUV as an incoming call, they both froze for a moment.

But Micah hit the answer button.

Before he could even say hello, Krystal whispered, "If you happen to know where Berkley is, she's wanted for questioning in the murder of her ex-husband. Tell her to come to the station but only with a lawyer and not to say a *word* without said lawyer."

The line went dead.

"You think she knows I'm with you?"

"Yeah." His grim tone mirrored exactly how she was feeling.

Chapter 11

DESPITE THE ICE-COLD INTERROGATION room, sweat slicked down Berkley's spine. She was glad to have on a jacket though—to hide the sweat pools under her armpits.

She'd arrived two hours ago with Micah, and her lawyer was supposed to have met her, but she'd just been alone in here. Waiting.

She knew the detectives in charge were likely watching her via the two-way mirror in the wall and she didn't have her phone to distract her. Or have it as a way to contact Micah to see what the hell was going on and where her lawyer was.

Since they hadn't told her not to leave, she decided to get up and go find a bathroom. Mostly just to have something else to do. But the minute she reached the door, two detectives she vaguely recognized opened it from the other side.

"Sorry to keep you waiting," the first said. He was in his fifties with a bushy gray beard that sort of reminded her of Santa Claus.

The other detective was a younger man. Maybe in his thirties. Good-looking. And he didn't say anything. Just stood next to the mirror behind the table while Santa Claus sat down across from where she'd been sitting.

"Where's my lawyer?" she asked. Because she knew enough not to say a damn word without her lawyer present.

Santa—she needed to know his name—opened a manila file that likely had nothing to do with whatever this was about, and shuffled some stuff around. "He's checking in but we thought we'd just wait here with you until he finished up at the front."

Okay so Santa was going to act like a bumbling fool. Great.

"First we'd like to thank you for coming in of your own accord."

She simply nodded because she wasn't a hundred percent sure what they knew. Obviously they knew about Henry—something she was still trying to process. Her sister had told Micah that he was murdered.

Now she was glad she hadn't seen him on the bed. Not because she was worried about leaving forensic evidence behind, but because despite everything, she didn't think she could handle seeing him...like that.

Of course her mind went to the absolute worst-case scenario, filling in all the blanks. But then she wondered if he'd been killed in the same manner as James Reed. Which would make sense since it seemed highly likely that the same person had dumped her at both places.

"Let's talk about why you're here."

"Without my lawyer?" she asked.

The man behind Santa Claus cleared his throat.

"Right, of course," Santa said with a chuckle.

"Also, you two haven't even introduced yourselves. Are you detectives?"

Santa's gaze sharpened on her then, maybe realizing that she wasn't naïvely going to play his game.

"Detective Dylan Levitz," the younger man said, his tone even and soothing, like one of those ASMRtists who lulled you to sleep by their voice alone.

"And I'm Detective Sean Dewey. But you can just call me Dewey." He glanced at his watch, frowned. "Are you hungry? Thirsty? I just realized how long you've been in here."

"I'm good, but thank you." She didn't want food—didn't trust herself not to hurl—she wanted to leave. Or to at least get this thing over with. If she was going to jail, she'd like to know sooner than later.

Dewey's jaw ticked once, but he didn't lose that easy expression she was sure had lulled plenty of people into feeling like they could open up to him. Under different circumstances, she probably would have too. Or if she hadn't already had more than enough experience to last a lifetime with law enforcement, she wouldn't have pushed for her lawyer.

She'd have trusted his stupid Santa Claus face.

Young her had been dumb. Or maybe just inexperienced.

"Let's talk about why you're here."

"Okay." She thought about asking for her lawyer again, but held back. These two hadn't read her rights to her or even told her what they wanted to talk to her about. So she could at least sit here and listen.

Detective Dewey (which sounded stupid, as if he'd walked off some show from the fifties), just watched her.

So she watched him right back. She'd grown up with three brothers and one sister and knew how to win a staring contest. Being a younger sibling had some advantages.

Levitz finally took a step forward but didn't sit. Just loomed over the table, his dark gaze laser sharp. "Let's talk about where you were last night."

"Why does that matter? Am I under arrest for something?" *Keep it vague and keep asking questions.*

"Who told you to come in here today? Was it your sister, Detective Knight?" Dewey asked.

Before she could even think about answering, the other detective spoke. "I'm more interested in your relationship with your ex-husband. And whether or not your sister called or texted you." Levitz seemed a little smarter than Dewey because he wasn't technically asking her questions, just making statements.

But at this point they weren't even being subtle, and it pissed her off. They wanted her to say something and slip up. "I've asked for my lawyer multiple times. I'm not talking without them." She stood, but paused when Levitz went as if to grab his weapon.

She held up her palms. "Seriously?" That was when she realized he was making a move for his cuffs, not gun. But still.

"Come on now, just have a seat." Dewey was still sitting down, completely unruffled.

"Am I under arrest?" she asked.

"Not yet."

"Then I'm free to leave?" She'd come in here of her own accord, but it was clear they were trying to get her to talk without her lawyer, so she was going to make them arrest her. They'd have forty-eight hours to do something about her arrest and then be forced to let her go. And given the direction of their questioning, she didn't think they had enough to arrest her.

Or more importantly, to get a search warrant.

She hated that she couldn't contact Micah to find out what he knew. This could be the wrong move, but she wanted to force them into action.

Before either of them responded, a statuesque woman in a dark black skirt suit that probably cost more than Berkley's car strode in, her long, platinum blonde hair and heart-shaped face what men wrote odes about.

And to her utter surprise, Nick Storm was right behind the woman, his expression dark.

"Berkley Knight, don't say a word to these men," the woman said. "Sinead Goode entering the interrogation room, where I would like to note that two detectives are questioning my client without her representation."

This wasn't the lawyer she'd called from Micah's phone. This was...oh. Ooooh hell, she recognized the name, if not the woman's face. Sinead Goode was some big-time criminal attorney who'd represented a handful of well-known cases that made national news. Including one of a woman suspected of murdering her husband—and Goode had gotten her off, if Berkley remembered correctly.

She wondered who the lawyer was making a note to, but then saw the little red light on in the camera in the corner of the room. Oh, she was officially documenting herself. Had the camera always been on? Clearly Berkley wasn't paying as much attention as she should.

Dewey stood, and gone was the easygoing detective as he stared Sinead Goode down. "No need to get all twisted."

"Ms. Knight, please come with me. You're not saying another word until we've had a chance to talk—in private." She gave a pointed look at the camera. "Because I don't trust them not to record our conversation."

Detective Levitz frowned. "Now see here—"

But his partner held up a hand and gave Berkley a look that sent a chill down her spine. "It's all right. Let her talk to her lawyer. We'll get what we want. We always do." With that, he strode from the room.

Before Berkley could think about talking, her lawyer motioned for her to follow.

She gave Nick a curious look, but his expression was granite as he followed after her, flanking her. As if protecting her.

For some reason, she liked that he was here, even if she had a dozen questions. Probably more.

They ended up in a quiet office that belonged to...one of the higher-ups for sure, since it had a window. This actually looked like the sheriff's office, but she'd never been in here so couldn't be sure.

"Ms. Knight—"

"Berkley's fine," she murmured. "And you're my lawyer?"

Sinead Goode smiled softly, a stark difference from the shark in the interrogation room. "I am, if you accept my representation. And you can call me Sinead. Before we go over anything else, what did you tell them?"

"Nothing."

"Nothing at all?"

Berkley recapped the non-conversation, and got a surprised but approving look from the lawyer. "Okay this is good. Very good. They've got nothing on you. Nothing but suspicion because your ex-husband was murdered and you're his ex-wife."

She winced slightly. "So he's really dead?" She'd known what Krystal had said to Micah, and what she'd seen in Henry's house but still...the reality was different. The *knowing*.

"He is," the woman said.

"Who...called you? I know your name and I kind of doubt I can afford you, so if you want to let my other lawyer—"

"Your fees are taken care of so don't even worry about that. Unless you have an objection, I'm your lawyer of record."

Berkley glanced at Nick, who'd given her his back and was staring out the window that overlooked the parking lot. She wanted to ask him what the hell he was doing here and if he was paying for her lawyer but that was crazy. She knew that much.

Maybe he was friends—or more?—with the high-priced lawyer. More than likely Micah had called in one of his infamous favors. She'd talk to him later. Damn it, she really needed her cell phone.

"I don't have an objection and thank you. I'm just...this is a lot to take in. This morning has been..." Oh god, her voice cracked and she had to fight back tears as the reality of her situation crashed in on her. "Sorry," she muttered. "I don't even know where to begin."

"Let's start with why you're here. Because I know you came in voluntarily. Everything you say is privileged, and if you want Mr. Storm to leave, I'll kick him out." She almost looked a little giddy at the thought, or maybe that was just amusement in her expression.

Berkley couldn't tell.

Nick turned around at that and glowered at Sinead, but the woman was unaffected by his glare. Just sniffed imperiously.

"No, he can stay." Berkley couldn't look at him again even as she wondered what the hell he was doing here. She should probably feel more vulnerable with him here, but he made her feel safer in a way she couldn't explain.

"Okay. Then start at the beginning." Sinead's voice was soft, encouraging.

For a moment she almost told her about James Reed, but decided to just stick to the facts of the night before. She and Micah were the only ones who knew what happened in regard to Reed and she wasn't sure she trusted anyone else. So she recapped how she'd woken up this morning and run straight to her brother's place. She went right up until she saw the cops outside her house and left out the part about Krystal calling Micah. No need to get her sister in trouble.

Because those detectives had each asked about Krystal, so something more was going on there.

"I was freaked out seeing all those flashing lights, so my brother and I headed straight to the police station." She looked at Nick, who'd moved in next to her and was leaning against the desk. "How'd you know I was here?"

"Clover told me."

That answered something else that she'd been wondering about.

He frowned at her. "Wait, didn't you tell her you were here?"

Nope, not touching that. She was no snitch, and if Micah and Clover had a thing going on, she wasn't telling Nick.

She turned back to the lawyer. "Should I tell the cops the truth?"

"Not if they don't ask for it. Not yet anyway. In fact, you're not saying a damn word to them. I'm still waiting to find out when Mr. Moore's time of death was."

"Why...oh, right. Do you know how..." She cleared her throat. "How he was killed?"

"Sharp force trauma to the neck."

Just like James Reed. She shivered and was surprised when Nick placed a gentle hand over hers and squeezed. But she also didn't hate it.

"Henry has cameras at his house."

"If they had you on camera, you'd be in cuffs." There was no give in the woman's tone as she stood. "Sit tight," she said as she glanced at her phone and stepped out of the room.

Once it was just the two of them, Berkley glanced at Nick to find him watching her with a mix of emotions.

"Do you know if my brother is here? Ah, Micah? And what about Krystal? I haven't seen her."

"All your siblings are in the lobby. They're fit to be tied." His expression was still difficult to read. The man would have made a great attorney.

She blinked. "Can I call one of them using your phone?"

"Of course." He held out his phone with ease.

Instead of calling Krystal, because she didn't want to put her in an awkward position—and also, she was nervous about talking to her—she called Micah.

"It's me," she said when he answered. "I'm using Nick Storm's phone."

"Are you okay?"

"I think so." She told him what was going on, then said, "Is there anything I need to know?"

"They don't have access to your house," he whispered as a horn honked in the background and she figured he'd gone outside the station to talk. "No warrant. But it seems like they're trying hard to get one."

"Do you know why?"

"Other than you being the ex-wife? Apparently you sent him some threatening emails?"

"Wait, what! No I didn't!" She was being framed. But who would hate her that much?

"Yeah, that's what I figured. Hopefully these dumbass detectives will figure it out, but if not, your new attorney has an incredible investigator on her payroll."

"Really?"

"Oh yeah. The absolute best. I'm going to dig more myself now that I know what bullshit they've got. And if I had to guess, someone spoofed your email address or just created one that looks close enough to yours."

She had more questions, but didn't want to ask too many in front of Nick. Seriously, why was he here? She understood that Clover had told him, but that didn't explain his presence. "How's Krystal? Is this going to affect her job or anything?" she asked Micah.

He started to answer, but suddenly Krystal was on the line. "How are you? Are you okay? Did those bastards screw with you? I'll murder Dewey." There was pure rage in her voice.

"I'm fine. They were just doing their job." That was debatable, but she didn't want her sister getting worked up. "I'm more worried about you. Will this affect your cases or—"

"Oh my god, stop. I'm a grown woman. That's why I'm not officially talking to you about anything right now. Here's Micah," she murmured before her brother came back on the line.

"Everyone's good. Just keep your mouth shut—because Henry's cameras were turned off last night."

She wasn't sure how she felt about that. One on hand, it was good for her because she'd been able to escape without being seen. But clearly someone was setting her up. She just had no idea why. She had no real enemies that she could think of.

Once they disconnected, she handed the phone back to Nick, but still felt lost, untethered from everything.

"Did your brother say anything about your blood test?" Nick asked.

Damn it, she'd forgotten to ask. She shook her head.

He stood again, paced to the window, his big body almost vibrating with rage. "You were with me until midnight last night, so if—"

Her lawyer stepped into the room then, cutting him off. "You're free to go."

"Wait, what?" Berkley said.

"TOD is eleven o'clock last night. You couldn't have done it. Nick will be making a statement, verifying your alibi," she said, looking at him pointedly. "And I've already given them the name of the restaurant you two were at. I'm sure the annoyed staff will remember the two of you."

She nodded, feeling a little in shock. "What about...what I told you?"

"Hold on to that for now. We're going to tell them, but I want to get you out of here right now. You've likely been drugged and you're in shock. I want you to go home, get a shower and reset. They've already proven they don't respect the law by trying to talk to you without your lawyer. We're not going to do them any favors. Your job is not to solve your ex-husband's murder. That's on them." There was steel in Sinead's voice. "Also I need your email address. However many you have. Work ones, personal ones."

"Is this because of the alleged angry emails I sent him?" At the lawyer's look she said, "I talked to my brother while you were gone. He filled me in."

The woman nodded. "Yes. I've seen the emails and they're...calculated. The wording feels off to me. Either way, I've got my investigator working to track down who sent them, but I need your addresses."

"You're fast," Berkley murmured, even as she started scribbling down all her email addresses. She had four. Two personal and two for work.

She also realized the woman was right about getting out of here. She wasn't sure that she was actually in shock, but she couldn't be at this station another second longer or she'd start screaming. Her ex-husband had been murdered, someone was trying to frame her for it, and...her emotions about his death were complicated. At one point she'd thought she wanted him dead, had hated him so deeply. But now... She shook off the dark thought. "I need to find out who's trying to set me up."

Sinead nodded even as Nick placed a steady hand at the small of her back. His touch anchored her, made her feel less alone even as she told herself that was stupid. He was simply here to provide an alibi.

In the lobby she found all of her siblings, even Krystal, who hung back from the others while everyone hugged her. Her sister simply nodded at Berkley, relief in her gaze as she eyed her, before heading back into the station.

"I'm going to give the cops my statement," Nick said and disappeared back inside.

She still wasn't sure why he was there and hadn't had time to ask him before her three brothers whisked her out of the lobby and into Apollo's SUV.

She wanted to call him, thank him, but...then second-guessed herself. Her lawyer was right. She needed a shower and to reset from all this.

Then figure out who the hell hated her enough to murder two people and set her up for it.

Chapter 12

"So you ever gonna tell me why you called in this particular favor?" Sinead asked, eyebrows raised.

Nick stopped with her at the driver's side of her black Navigator. "Favors mean you're supposed to do what's asked without questions."

She snort-laughed, looking like the girl he'd grown up with for a moment and not the badass lawyer who made grown men cry on the stand. Or on a random Tuesday. "I thought we were friends. And the vibe between you two was...I don't know. *Interesting*."

He tried to find the right words to answer, then sighed. "I don't know why I called you. I mean, I know why, you're the best."

"Damn straight."

When Clover called him this morning, worried about Berkley, he'd simply gone with his instinct. And that wasn't a normal reaction for him. He didn't just *react* to things; he thought things out, weighed any ramifications. But his only instinct had been to protect Berkley. If she hadn't been with him at the time of the murder, he'd have lied, been her alibi. And that knowledge shook him to his core.

"Well?" Sinead was still watching him.

"I wanted to make sure she was okay, that's all. Something like this could get out of control fast without the right lawyer." He lifted a shoulder, trying to appear casual when he felt anything but.

Because he was still keyed up at the way those assholes had trapped Berkley in that interrogation room. She'd asked for a lawyer more than once but they hadn't cared. That told him all he needed to know about the detectives.

"You want to protect her."

"Well yeah."

Sinead gave him a smile he couldn't read, then unlocked her vehicle but still didn't make a move to get inside. "I've got Vera already looking into things. It's clear someone has an axe to grind with your woman and it's going to get worse before it gets better."

His woman? He didn't hate the thought of it.

"Make sure she always has an alibi if you can. Someone needs to be with her at all times—she's got siblings and friends. Work that shit out. And in the meantime, I'll do what I do best."

"Are you going to tell the cops the rest of what happened?" Or more likely have Berkley make an official statement once the shock wore off.

"We'll see what plays out. She has no legal duty to make a statement, and my job is to protect her. You just need to keep your woman safe."

Berkley wasn't his woman, but he wasn't going to negate his friend's words.

"Oh," she said as she slid into the driver's seat. "Bring her food. Feed her. Cook for her. Show her that you're actually useful and more than a pretty face." Her grin was pure Sinead before she shut the door in his face.

It wasn't like he needed instructions on how to...what, pursue or court a woman? Because yeah, that was what he wanted to do. More than his next breath. But more than that, he just wanted to keep Berkley safe right now until the real killer was caught. Because she was in clear danger. Someone wanted to hurt her. But not physically. Not yet anyway. They were screwing with her, wanted her locked up. That was…diabolical. Calculated.

As he pulled out of the parking lot of the sheriff's department, he called Clover.

"Hey. Everything okay?" she asked as she answered on the first ring.

"Yeah, just leaving now. Are you with Berkley? How is she?"

"Ah, I'm not currently with her, but she's at home with her brothers. And I think she's still processing everything. Which is obviously understandable."

Yeah, regardless of them being divorced, he doubted she'd wanted the man murdered. On top of that, someone was clearly trying to hurt her, to set her up for murder. Had drugged her in her own home. That was beyond psychotic. Whoever this was, wasn't just going to give up. Something he was sure Berkley understood. But Sinead was right, she shouldn't be alone. She needed to be with someone at all times. Not just for an alibi, but for protection.

Even on the job when she was working for him and Clover. She couldn't be alone at that mansion or just working with her assistant. Nope, he was going to put some protections in place.

"So how did you find out about everything?" Because Berkley had been surprised when he'd mentioned Clover's name. "Berkley didn't tell you." It was a guess, but a good one.

"Oh shoot, I'm getting another call. Byyyeee." She hung up before he could respond.

Which answered one of his questions. His sister was seeing one of the Knight brothers. He just wasn't sure which one.

He'd deal with that later. For now, he needed to pick up a few things, make some calls, then head straight to Berkley's place.

***

Nick knocked on Berkley's door, glad she had a door camera and another visible one in the corner of the patio ceiling.

Berkley was clearly surprised to see him when she answered her front door. Probably because he hadn't called ahead.

"Did you check the cameras before answering?" he asked her.

She blinked at his brusque, demanding tone. "Ah, yes, of course. What are you doing here?"

He held up the plethora of bags. "Making you dinner." Then he strolled into her house as if he had every right to be there. He definitely should have called, but he hadn't wanted to risk her telling him not to come over. He wasn't used to these feelings, this tight sensation in his chest every time he was close to her. And knowing that someone was actively trying to harm her... He needed to keep her safe.

"Wait..." Sighing, she shut and locked the front door behind him.

"Who else is here? I brought enough to cook for your brothers too."

Faint surprise flickered in her green eyes. "Cormac is out getting food—and Apollo is currently sitting across the street. His vibe was too intense and I just needed a few minutes to myself." Her tone was defensive, as if she'd had more than one argument with her brothers.

She also didn't say where Micah was, but he didn't ask.

"Did you at least set your alarm?"

"Oh my god, I have three brothers, I don't need another one." With an exasperated sound she turned away from him and stalked toward what turned out to be her kitchen.

He definitely didn't want to take on a brother role, but he kept his mouth shut because she hadn't kicked him out yet. And he wasn't going to give her a chance to.

"What kind of food did you bring?" She looked more than mildly curious as she eyed all his bags.

"I'm going to make spaghetti bolognese." Unless she kicked him out too.

"That sounds amazing. I'm glad my brothers aren't here to eat it all," she muttered. Then frowned at him. "Why are you being so nice to me?"

"Should I not be nice to you?"

"You're…cooking for me." And it sounded like an accusation. "After showing up as my alibi and bringing me a high-powered lawyer."

"A true alibi." Wasn't like he'd been lying. Though he certainly would have. Something he decided to keep to himself.

She sniffed slightly, eyeing him like she wasn't sure what he was up to, so he turned away and started pulling out ingredients.

Cooking was something he could do well, and from the time he was young it had been one of his mental escapes. Even his asshole of a father hadn't had shit to say about the meals he'd made for the family.

"So how are you doing?" he asked as he started prepping. "With Henry's death? It's got to be a lot to deal with."

She pulled out the pots and pans he would need as well as the bottle of wine he'd brought. "You're the only person to ask me that," she murmured as she popped the cork. "And I don't know. I despised him by the end. Once I saw his true self, the man he'd been hiding behind the mask, I realized that I never loved *him*, but the illusion of him. After that, it was…I don't know. I wouldn't say easy to leave, but it wasn't hard. And he hated me for that, I think. He hated that I saw through him and had no feelings anymore." She snorted, seeming to be more talking to herself than him. "I actually think he just hated women in general but…" Clearing her throat, she shook her head. "I don't know how I am, and that's all I've got."

"Fair enough. Look, I'm sure you know this, but someone is targeting you."

"I know. I just…can't imagine who. Honestly. Someone who hates me enough to kill t—" She cleared her throat again, took a sip of her wine. "Thank you for this. Especially since I missed my first day of work for you." Her tone was wry.

"I'm not worried about that at all." He added the pasta to the boiling water. "But I am curious which of your brothers my sister is dating."

She blinked at him, her green eyes going wide for a moment. "I don't know that she actually is dating one of them."

He narrowed his gaze at her.

Which just made her smile.

And man, he loved that smile. It really was like the sun coming out.

Just as quickly, it dimmed at the sound of a chime from her phone. He recognized it because he used the same doorbell app at home.

"I'll grab it." He moved fast before she could protest. He doubted someone coming to attack her would use the doorbell, but he wasn't taking the chance.

She made an exasperated sound behind him, but he didn't hear her stool scrape against the floor so figured she was staying put.

"It's my friends," she called out as he reached the foyer. "I can see them on camera."

Some of the tension in his shoulders eased but he still checked the peephole anyway before opening the door. Sure enough, two of her friends stood there, one he recognized from last night.

They both stared at him once he opened the door.

The shorter of the two—Silvia, he remembered—moved first. She stepped into the house, the tall one following. "Where is she?" Silvia demanded, glaring up at him, as if he'd had anything to do with what was going on.

The blonde glared at him too.

"Kitchen."

The two women dismissed him before hurrying into the kitchen. Before locking up, he stepped outside and scanned her front yard and street.

She lived in a quiet neighborhood near the end of a cul-de-sac. He'd seen enough kids' bikes and other toys in some of the front yards to see that this was a family-friendly neighborhood. Nothing looked out of the ordinary, but... Yep, he spotted Apollo sitting in a truck across the street under an oak tree.

The shadows mostly hid the vehicle, a perfect spot.

He raised his hand in a wave before ducking back inside and locking up. At least her brother waved back. He wondered when Cormac would be back.

He passed Berkley and her friends, who were now in her living room, all talking in hushed whispers, and headed back to the kitchen.

Until she kicked him out—and he hoped that she didn't—he was going to feed her and keep her safe.

Chapter 13

"WHAT IS HE DOING here? Are you guys like..." Silvia made a thrusting motion with her hips.

Berkley let out a burst of laughter, the sound a little rusty. "Oh my god, no. No, no, no. He's my alibi for last night, and oh my god you guys, I seriously don't know what's going on." She hadn't told them everything. Normally she would, but she didn't have the energy to repeat everything. And Micah was right. She needed to keep that circle small.

Nick Storm now knew way more than she'd ever imagined telling him—even though she hadn't told him everything. And she was pretty sure he was paying for her attorney. He hadn't denied it when she'd accused him of bringing in the high-powered attorney—and her family hadn't hired Sinead. That left him. Or maybe he was dating Sinead... She didn't want to think about him and the tall blonde, so she shut that tab down.

"I can't believe the dumbass cops arrested you," Silvia growled. "And that we had to hear it from Krystal."

"Yeah, what the hell?" Kendall demanded.

"First, I can't believe my sister called you," Berkley said.

"She assumed we knew." Silvia's look was pointed.

"Fine, I should have told you both. But I'm still processing everything," she whisper-yelled. "This *just* happened. I haven't had a chance to just sit down and think." She'd seen Nick head back to the kitchen. Since he was making a little noise, she assumed he was still cooking.

That by itself was surreal. A man she'd had a few fantasies about—both sexual and in the realm of punching him in his face—was in her kitchen, cooking for her.

What the hell was happening in her life? None of this felt real! Someone was trying to set her up for murder—multiple murders. Her ex-husband was dead. Someone had poisoned her or drugged her or something, and now Nick Storm was in her house looking more gorgeous than any man had a right to. While cooking her dinner.

Nothing made sense.

"How are you doing?" Silvia's voice was gentler now as she sat next to her on the couch.

"Yeah. And seriously, why is Nick Storm here...cooking?" Kendall glanced at the entryway in the direction of the kitchen even though they couldn't see him from the living room.

"I'm...dealing. And I have no idea."

"You have no idea?" Kendall's tone was disbelieving.

"No," she snapped with more force than she'd intended. She winced as guilt swamped her. Her friends had shown up because they loved her. She couldn't take out her bullshit on them. "Sorry. I'm trying to process everything and I think I just need sleep."

"Well, we're staying the night," Kendall said, no give in her voice.

"No, you both have jobs and... Two of my brothers are coming back later anyway." Also, she really didn't want her friends in danger. She'd already changed the security code at least, so she'd be safe tonight.

Tomorrow...she was thinking about her options. She loved her home, didn't want to be run out of it, but she was starting to think that she needed a little distance. She wanted to be able to think her options through when her mind was clearer, not be reactive.

That was how the younger Berkley handled things. By reacting without thinking. She wanted to be smart about dealing with this...nightmare. That was the only word she could think of to call this.

All her brothers had offered her their places to stay, and she knew Krystal would take her in even if it was some sort of conflict of interest. At this point she had an alibi so there should be no conflict, but she wasn't sure if the sheriff's department would see it that way. Speaking of, she really needed to talk to Krystal.

Her friends gently argued with her for about ten minutes, but eventually relented and just kept her company until she walked them both out. By that point, the house smelled amazing and her stomach was already rumbling. That was when she realized she hadn't eaten...all day.

When she saw Apollo sitting in his truck across the street, she jogged over to see him. She thought he would just park in her driveway and catch up on work emails or something.

He rolled down his window. "Hey, get in here, it's cold."

"Why don't you just come inside instead?" Even if she'd been looking forward to spending some alone time with Nick, something she would never ever say out loud.

"I'm officially un-banished from the house?"

"Ha ha. And yes. Sorry, I just... it's been a lot and I needed quiet. Can you text Cormac though, tell him not to come back? I mean, obviously say it nicer than that?" She could only deal with one brother at a time right now.

"Nothing to be sorry for. And I already told him I had tonight covered. Figured I'd just order us food anyway." As he grabbed his bag from the back, he said, "What's Storm doing here?"

"Nick? Ah, cooking dinner for me."

He frowned down at her. "Why?"

"What do you mean, why? It's almost dinner time."

He made an exasperated sound. "All right, smart-ass. Are you two dating?"

"Nope." And that was all she was going to say about that. She had no idea why the man was here so she certainly couldn't explain it to her very nosy, very protective brother.

In the kitchen, she realized Nick hadn't been kidding about having enough food for her brothers.

Nick and Apollo did that thing guys do and sort of sized each other up. But then to her surprise, Apollo grinned when he realized what Nick was making.

"You're making spaghetti bolognese? Hell yeah. I'll make a salad." Apollo grabbed some salad stuff from the fridge and started making three individual ones as Nick plated the food for them.

Seriously, everything about this was so surreal. Apollo was being all normal and kind of nice with Nick in the kitchen, making small talk and... She was just going to eat and crash and deal with everything tomorrow.

Because this was too much.

"I was thinking that you should mention to either Sinead or the cops...or your sister that Silvia was at the restaurant last night too. God, was it only last night?" Nick muttered, but then shook his head.

"Wait, what?" Apollo, sitting across from them at her kitchen table, looked between them.

"Oh, Silvia was there on a date or something." Berkley still wanted to know who Silvia had been dating the last couple months, but that was low on her priorities right now. "And you're right," she said to Nick. "It'll shore up my alibi even more." And she didn't trust those detectives not to come at her again.

"So are you staying tonight?" Nick asked, now focusing that granite expression on her brother. "Because she shouldn't be alone right now."

"*She* is sitting right here," Berkley said in annoyance.

They both ignored her as Apollo straightened slightly in his seat. They were both large men, with Apollo being about six foot four, a couple inches taller than Nick.

Nick didn't look the least bit intimidated.

"I don't answer to you." Apollo's voice was calm, and that wasn't always a good thing with him. He'd been in military intelligence for years, had a level head in most situations. Which just meant she'd seen him clock someone when stone-cold relaxed.

"I know that. But your sister is in danger."

"I'm literally right here." Also, the bolognese was so good she didn't even care that they were literally talking about her as if they couldn't hear her. Whatever, she started devouring the food and forced herself not to moan at how good it was. Okay, so Nick was gorgeous and could cook—well. And he'd charged to her defense without her even asking.

She really didn't want to like that so much.

"I know that too," Apollo growled. "Do you really think that we all didn't try to get her to come home with us? She's just stubborn. I'm staying the night and my brothers will take shifts the rest of the week if necessary. This is really good, by the way."

And that was that. Nick nodded, either at the compliment or that Apollo was staying here, she wasn't sure. Maybe both. "Thanks. I'll stay on the street, keep an eye on things so you have backup."

She didn't want Nick to have to stay out there in his car in the cold all night. "Can you guys see and hear me? Am I a ghost? Is this the afterlife?"

They both looked at her and she forced herself to look at Apollo instead of Nick. Otherwise she was going to get swallowed up in his storm gray eyes. His last name really was fitting.

"We hear you," Apollo said, his tone softer than she'd ever heard it.

She didn't like it. Oh no, she wanted the brother who called her dumbass back.

"And you are stubborn," he added.

Well, facts were facts. "Whatever," she muttered and dug into her food.

She couldn't deal with her brother and Nick at the same time, especially when she was so off-balance.

Mostly, she couldn't handle the fact that Nick was being so nice to her. And she was starting to think that maybe...he wasn't so awful after all.

Chapter 14

BERKLEY SAT UP FROM a deep sleep, adrenaline punching through her as her house alarm pierced the air.

Trying not to panic, she grabbed her phone from the nightstand, ready to call the cops, then Apollo strode into her room, pistol in hand. He held a finger to his mouth and directed her to the bathroom.

"Don't turn off the alarm," he ordered.

She hadn't been planning to, even though the shrill tone was taking over everything to the point she could barely hear his instructions. Before she could respond, he raced out as she crouched down in the bathtub, heart pounding.

Her phone rang, the name of her security company on the caller ID. She answered it but couldn't make out anyone on the other line so hung up. She called 911, but also couldn't hear anything so hung up on them too.

The cops would be on the way now regardless, but all she could focus on was her brother. She had a pistol in a safe in her closet—a gift from Apollo years ago—but there was no way she could risk getting it now.

She knew her brother was smart and trained but fear bled into her bones as she imagined every horrible scenario. Someone had been skilled enough to abduct her from her own home in the middle of the night. Her brother wasn't infallible. What if someone got the drop on him?

As the seconds ticked by, she crept out of the bathtub and grabbed a couple things from underneath her sink as a weapon. A big-ass can of hairspray and a lighter. Not much, but she could mess someone up with them. Or at least take them off guard with a big burst of flame straight in their face.

Then suddenly everything went quiet—only to be followed by a loud crash.

Heart in her throat, she jumped up and raced out of her room. Slowing her pace, she eased down the hallway.

"You're replacing this." That was Apollo.

"I couldn't get the door open." Now Nick.

"So you just kicked it in?" Apollo demanded.

Okay, if they were talking, then they were fine. She hurried down and found the two of them in the foyer, her front door kicked in. Apparently by Nick. The frame was splintered and the table behind the door was cracked, the knickknacks on it scattered on the wood flooring in the entryway.

Nick moved fast, covering the distance between them in seconds as he tucked his weapon away.

In the distance she heard at least one siren.

"What are you doing here?" She looked past him at the destroyed door-frame. He'd said he'd be staying in his truck across the street, but she hadn't thought he'd actually stay the whole night. Maybe just an hour or two max.

"Your boyfriend here kicked in the door," Apollo grumbled without much heat.

She ignored the boyfriend comment—so did Nick.

"I saw someone running away from your house when the alarm system went off," he said. "I chased them to the backyard but they were fast, *fast*. Jumped the fence and I was more worried about you, so I came back."

"You could've come in the side door. It's the one your would-be intruder entered from," Apollo said, snark in his tone.

Her gut twisted at the knowledge that someone had broken into her place again. She'd known it was a possibility but...whoever was after her was bold. And that was even more dangerous.

"I obviously didn't know that..." Nick took a breath and looked Berkley over in a clinical fashion. "Are you hurt at all?"

"No. But someone broke in?" The sirens were louder now and she wanted answers before the cops arrived. Normally she had a thirty-second delay on her security system, but when she'd changed the code, she'd also changed the delay to only five seconds after last night. Now she was glad she had. "Was it a man or woman?" She had cameras and needed to check the feed.

"I couldn't tell. They were tall, athletic...and fast. Whoever it was had on a thick-looking puffer jacket. Dark color. And puffy ski-style pants. Under oath, I couldn't say if it was a woman wearing bigger clothes or a bulky man. It was too dark, and like I said, they were sprinting."

"They picked your lock." Apollo's voice was grim.

She headed toward the door she used to enter her house most days. Right next to her parking area. She didn't have an actual garage, but a little paved area with a covering. She lived in an older area and garages weren't as common in her neighborhood. "Did you turn off the alarm?"

"Yeah," Apollo said. "But you can see that they tried to enter your old code."

She read the messages on the dashboard's inbox stating that she'd input the wrong code twice. Obviously not her, but someone had known the old code. Which explained how someone had taken her last night. Unfortunately that list of people was long—and that was on her for not being more vigilant. The law enforcement sirens were so loud they had to be in front of her house by now.

Nick disappeared as she looked at her brother.

Her stomach tightened as she spoke, needing to say this part out loud. "Someone who had this code must have tried to enter it. Right? That's the only explanation. Someone in my life tried to break into my house. Not a stranger. Your truck isn't in the driveway so they must have thought I was alone. When they didn't disarm the system within the time frame, they clearly ran." She wasn't sure where Nick had parked but she was guessing it wasn't in her driveway either.

If Henry hadn't been dead, he would have been her first suspect for breaking in. She didn't actually think he would, but on her list of people who hated her, he was number one. So yeah, he'd have been at the top of it. As it was…she still couldn't think of someone who'd done this. And that was disturbing. Hell, beyond terrifying. Some person was out there who hated her enough to commit murder…to try to set her up for murder. To break into her house, bold as you please.

"I can't stay here right now," she said more to herself as she pulled up her phone to look at her camera feeds. She had a few different exterior cameras, but before she could even press play on one of them, Apollo, big brother that he was, grabbed her phone and started scrolling through the feeds. She hated when he took over, but knew to pick her battles. "Your side camera isn't working."

She looked at the screen, saw the little square was grayed out and read *Camera is offline*. Great. Just freaking great.

Before she could respond, Nick strode in with two uniformed police officers in tow.

He'd probably explained some things to them, but she was definitely going to have to make a statement. She wasn't sure if she'd have to actually go down to the station for this kind of statement. Either way, she also needed to pack, because she wasn't coming back here until she knew she was safe.

Chapter 15

Nick was almost done for the day, but he had to make one more stop before he headed to the Carmine Mansion. To see Berkley. It had been over a day since someone had broken into her place, then run away like the coward they were. After this stop, he was going to convince her to stay with him.

Hopefully.

Though he wasn't sure what kind of chance he had at convincing her. Or if he even deserved it. Either way he still wanted to keep her safe. And her brothers were all bulldogs. Her sister too. He knew he'd have a fight on his hands trying to convince her to stay with him, but he was going to try anyway.

Because he couldn't sit back and do nothing while some maniac was out there targeting her.

Before he faced that battle, he had to face something Clover had brought up to him—rightfully yelled at him at brunch.

He parked at one of his many jobsites, then jogged up the steps to the work trailer, knocked briefly even as he opened it just to give Hannah notice he was here. No one normally knocked, but he knew what she'd been through with her abusive ex and he never wanted to startle her.

"Just me." He stepped into the meticulously neat trailer, and as always was impressed by how not only organized it was, but how good it smelled. Most of his jobsites just smelled like sweat and dirt.

"Mr. Storm." Her face lit up as she saw him and she started to stand from behind her desk where she was clearly busy.

"Sit, please." He strolled to the coffee and snacks station she'd set up, mostly for the crew. None of the other project managers did stuff like this and he didn't micromanage. But he liked what he saw here and how much her crew respected her. Half of them had already asked to be assigned to whatever next job she was on.

"Everything okay?"

"More than okay," he said as he poured a cup of coffee. "You're ahead of schedule. And I would say it's a miracle, but it's because you're efficient."

"Oh." She looked surprised, but smiled. "That's nice to hear, thank you."

"How's this crew working out?" He'd hand-picked them and knew they all worked well together, but he still wanted to check with her personally.

"Great. All hard workers, something I can't always say. But there are no slackers in this bunch."

"Good. Good." He took a sip of his coffee, looked around her personal space—

"Mr. Storm? What's going on?"

"What do you mean?" He focused on her now.

Her dark hair was pulled back in a braid, and she had on the standard flannel shirt and jeans mostly everyone wore around the jobsites. He knew she was in her forties, but she looked younger, and he figured that was because she'd lost the stress of her ex. Right now she was staring at him with dark, searching eyes.

"You've never stopped by to just chat, so come on. I'm closing up in fifteen and want to get out of here on time."

He let out a startled laugh. "A year ago you wouldn't have been that straight with me. I like it," he added when she frowned at him.

"Well, what's up, then?" Her chair creaked slightly as she leaned back and watched him. There was a confidence to her now that he loved seeing.

"I'm not sure how to say this, so I might screw it up."

She paled. "Are you firing me?"

"Wha—no! No, no, no." He scrubbed a hand over his face. "I'm screwing this up. Someone brought something to my attention recently. That I can be less than generous..." *Damn it.* He trailed off as he struggled to find the right words, something that was rare for him. But this was unchartered territory.

"I'm happy with my pay scale. More than, if I'm being honest. But if you're looking to give out raises, I'll take it." Her tone was pure snark and he loved it.

He half smiled. "It's not about that. But all of you will get a bonus when this job is over. Screw it, I'm just going to try and get it out. I think I was less than fair when you finally left Don."

She frowned at him now in real confusion and leaned forward. "What the hell are you talking about? You put me up in one of your rentals for free, helped me get back on my feet. And in exchange for nothing. You just did it."

"I don't mean monetarily." And now he was wondering if he should have come here at all. Maybe he shouldn't have put any of this on Hannah, should have just started working on himself going forward. But Clover's words kept rolling around in his head. "Did I ever make you feel like...you thought I judged you for not leaving him sooner?"

"No. Even if you had, no one could have judged me more than I did myself." Her tone was dry as she sat back again.

"Well, I thought I might have. And if I ever indicated I thought that, I'm sorry. I can only imagine how hard it was to live with him and feel like you had no options."

"Thank you for saying that. If I can be honest, I'm still unpacking every-thing. Emotionally, I mean. Why I stayed so long, why I let him hurt me—"

"You didn't let him. That's on him. He's the abuser."

She gave him another wry smile. "You sound like my therapist."

He hadn't known she was in therapy but was glad to know she was. "Smart therapist."

She nodded. "Whatever you're clearly feeling guilty about, please don't. I'm finally feeling settled. Happy, even. And I might have my first date since everything this upcoming weekend." Her cheeks flushed.

"I'm glad to hear that." It meant she was truly moving on.

She cocked an eyebrow. "No threats to him or anything? Because the whole crew knows and they're already plotting his demise if he screws up. It's just one date," she murmured, but he could see that she liked how overprotective they were.

"I was going to talk to Bear about it later, see if he knew who the guy was." Bear would give him aallll the gossip. Because the man liked to talk more than any other human Nick knew. Or would likely ever know.

She laughed as she shook her head. "You guys are the worst. And also the best," she added, her expression soft. "Look, I'm good and we're good. If you need to be absolved for any guilt you're feeling, I absolve you. I can even give you some Hail Marys or whatever."

"I'm not Catholic."

She grinned. "Neither am I."

He let out a startled laugh and some of the weight he'd been carrying around since that lunch with Clover lifted. Definitely not all of it. And he knew it shouldn't.

But still, he was on the right track.

Chapter 16

"Afternoon."

The rumble of Nick's deeper voice made Berkley jump, but she managed to stifle a scream as she turned around.

It had been a day and a half since the would-be break-in at her place, and she was still jumpy even in this three-story mansion where no one was getting in or out without her bodyguard downstairs. She'd been on the third floor most of the day, glad for the excuse to work and hide away from the world. She hadn't even realized how late it was until just now.

"Hey," she murmured, taking her earbuds out, trying not to drink in the sight of Nick.

He was wearing hefty work boots, well-worn jeans that molded to his impressive thighs, and an equally worn flannel shirt that did nothing to hide his biceps. Or the rest of his upper body. She really needed to stop ogling him.

He held up his palms. "I didn't mean to scare you. I thought you heard me stomping up the stairs."

She gave him a ghost of a smile. "I normally would have, but I was listening to an audiobook." She'd needed the escape. After making her statement yesterday morning, she'd headed to Apollo's house where he'd insisted she would be staying. But after one day and one night there...she was looking for an escape already. She didn't want to go home or anything, but she'd forgotten how overbearing her brother could be.

She'd thrown herself into work here at the Carmine Mansion all day, making note of potential historically important finds and also just fun things. There was a costume jewelry collection that the local museum might be interested in and some small paintings she needed to get authenticated.

"Arlo is still downstairs. He won't be leaving until you tell him to, or I do on any given day." Nick's expression was hard and she understood why.

"Thank you again for hiring him." Arlo handled security for some of the Storm family construction sites, and Nick had brought him on to keep an eye on things here.

You know, in case someone tried to *kill* her or drug and kidnap her again. Seriously, what was her life? She still hadn't processed what was going on. Or maybe she had. She'd accepted that this was the bullshit she had to deal with, even if she didn't understand why someone had targeted her. Being able to work today had helped with her stress at least.

"Also," she continued. "Thank you for fixing my front door."

He half smiled as he glanced around the third-floor bedroom, likely taking in all the Post-it notes she'd placed on many of the items. "I did destroy it."

"Yeah, well, with good reason. And sorry Apollo was kind of a dick to you." Her brother hadn't let up, which was weird. He'd been all normal after Nick had cooked for them, but then after she'd made her statement at the police station, he'd started up again, acting like an overprotective brother.

"I have a younger sister too," he murmured, leaning down to look at one of the Tiffany lamps.

"Well, I can't see you threatening to punch one of her boyfriends in the throat."

"He said that?"

"Oh...I guess you weren't there for that." She shook her head, then internally froze as she realized what she'd said. It wasn't like Nick was even her boyfriend, and she'd made a reference to that. She was tired and overstimulated. And fine, scared.

To her surprise, Nick laughed. "It's okay. And I've absolutely threatened a couple of Clover's boyfriends."

"I'm sure she loved that," Berkley said dryly.

He just snorted. Then, "I'm not rushing you, but are you close to being done for the day?"

She glanced at her phone, realized how late it had gotten. She also realized she hadn't eaten lunch. "I'm at a natural stopping point, so yeah. And I'll tell Arlo that if he ever needs to leave, he can just come find me."

Nick smiled, and it transformed the hard lines of his face. He really was annoyingly good-looking. And it was like he was throwing it in her face. Obviously he wasn't, but whatever. "Oh, he knows that. I just wanted to check on your progress... That's a lie. I wanted to check on you."

"Oh." She blinked. "Thank you."

"So you're staying with Apollo?"

"Yeah." She rolled her eyes, glad to be talking about that and not focusing on the weird sensation of knowing that Nick Storm was checking on her. That he...maybe cared. And that she kind of liked that—a lot more than she'd admit to anyone.

"That's a bad thing?"

"No." She slid her work gloves off before shutting the window she'd left open for extra ventilation. This was one of the cleaner rooms, but the accumulation of dust and that musty scent that came with homes that had been untouched for a while permeated everything. "I have a feeling I have a different relationship with my brothers than you do with Clover."

"How so?" he asked as they descended the first staircase.

This one was a cool, winding one, but she loved the main staircase that connected the first and second floor. It was grand, oversized and opened up onto a landing with a huge stained-glass window depicting Sanctuary Falls's biggest waterfall that was so beautiful it took her breath away.

"Ah, did your sister ever hit you in the face with a cutting board?" she asked. "Or did you try to cut her hair in her sleep? Or change the word 'the' to 'butts' in a term paper? Or..." She trailed off at his horrified expression and laughed. "Yeah, I've got three brothers and they're all lunatics. I mean, I'd burn down the world for any of them, but we tussled when we were younger and I've got the scars to prove it." They did too.

"Aren't you like five years younger than Apollo?"

"Yes, but the cutting board thing was to Cormac. He's only a year older than me—and he deserved it. He dumped one of my friends right before the prom. As in one day before."

"So he got a cutting board to the face?"

She eyed him as they reached the first floor. "I can't tell if you're judging me."

"I'm impressed more than anything. And a little scared."

She grinned. "Right answer. For the record, Cormac actually realized what a dick move he'd made and they ended up going to prom together as friends." He had a busted nose in all his pictures, but whatever. "What's that look?"

"I'm really wondering who changed the word 'the' to 'butts' in the term paper? And what happened afterward? I need details."

Feeling lighter than she had in the last twenty-four hours, she laughed. "Oh, that was all Micah. He was a freshman and Cormac was a senior. I've been sworn to secrecy though as to why he did it, so..." She shrugged. "But to answer your last question, the teacher realized that someone had messed with the paper and allowed Cormac to turn in another version." She paused. "I just realized that Cormac really does deserve a lot of the shit we do to him."

Nick laughed, the sound easy and deep, and she really didn't want to like it so much. But it settled in her bones, wrapped around her and... *No!* She had to stop this. She didn't want to like him so much. What had happened to the judgy jerk from before? She wanted him back!

Lies. She liked this version of him so much better and that scared her. Now he was a gorgeous man who cooked for her, hired a bodyguard for her, and was checking up on her safety. And he'd brought in a badass attorney to stop her from going to jail. Yeah, she really did like this version of him.

Once they'd locked up the house and said good-bye to Arlo, Nick cleared his throat.

"Look," he said. "This might be overkill, but I'm going to follow you to Apollo's place."

"Not overkill."

He seemed surprised by her response.

"Someone broke into my place and tried to pin my ex's murder on me." And you know, another murder. Something she was still sitting on. Partially because saying it out loud terrified her, but also…she didn't have an alibi for the time of that murder. What if the cops decided to pin it on her? That older detective had scared her and she wasn't taking the chance. "Not overkill. Thank you, I appreciate it."

Tension seemed to leave his shoulders as he nodded. Then he waited as she got into her vehicle—a 1969 peacock blue Bronco she'd discovered at one of her jobs and taken as payment instead of money at the end.

She wanted to ask him why he was being so nice but wasn't sure she wanted the answer. Maybe he felt guilty for being so cold to her for so long and was trying to make it up to her? She had a feeling that some of this was Clover's doing. Whatever the reason, she would take it.

***

"What the hell?" Berkley looked at her speedometer as the flashing red and blue lights went off behind her. It was only four, so not dark yet, but it would be sunset soon. She was already counting down to spring when the time changed and they'd get light much longer.

The sun was setting behind her, making it hard to see the man approaching her Bronco.

She rolled down her window, then tensed. What if this was a setup, someone trying to kill her—

"License and insurance please." The uniformed man didn't even bother with niceties or the standard question cops usually asked—*Do you know why I pulled you over?* He just got right to it.

"Ah sure. Can I ask why you pulled me over?"

"Speeding." His tone was brisk and she couldn't see his eyes thanks to his sunglasses.

She pulled her license from her wallet and said, "You guys have radar now?" Because she knew for a fact that the sheriff's department here didn't have it. The state patrol did.

He paused, giving her a hard look, but didn't respond.

She handed over her license, then gave him her insurance. Once he walked back to his vehicle, she quickly turned on her dashcam, because something about this stop was giving her bad vibes. She was surprised he didn't ask for her registration, but maybe that was coming next.

As she sat there, she texted Nick, wondering if he'd even see it. She'd lost him at a red light by accident. There had been nowhere for her to pull over safely so she'd just driven slowly, hoping he'd catch up soon. By now he'd probably see her on the side of the two-lane highway. She dropped a pin just in case, because she was internally starting to freak out.

She shouldn't have stopped. But...what was she doing to do? Run from the cops?

A few minutes later the man dressed in uniform returned with her license and insurance, but was still holding on to them. "Do you have any weapons in the car?"

She started to say no, but then remembered... "I have pepper spray in my purse."

"Anything else?"

"No."

"Have you been drinking at all today?"

"No."

"Where are you coming from?"

"Work."

"And what do you do?"

She gave him a brief explanation, got a frown, then he said, "Can I search your vehicle?"

She wanted to say yes to get this over with, but that was going to be a hard hell no. "No, I don't consent to my vehicle being searched."

Now he paused for a long moment, just staring hard at her with those annoying reflective sunglasses. He had to be wearing them to intimidate her because it was too dark to need them at this point.

At a brief honk, they both turned. The officer tensed and strode away from her still holding on to her stuff.

Even though she hated calling her sister for help, she shoved down her discomfort and called Krystal. If anyone could find out if this cop was legit, it'd be her sister.

"Hey, how was your first day at the mansion? And how are you feeling?" Krystal asked immediately.

"Ah, fine. Listen, a cop I don't recognize pulled me over and asked to search my vehicle."

"What? Do not consent."

"I know, I know. I already said no," she murmured as she looked in the rearview mirror. That was when she realized someone had parked.

Oh shit. It was Nick.

No, no, no. She didn't want him getting into anything because of her. And pulling up behind a cop was bad news.

"I'll call you right back." She hung up before her sister could respond.

Her phone rang immediately so she silenced it, but leaned out the driver's window and took a picture of the guy's cop car and sent it to Krystal. Then she texted, *everything okay, Nick is here. Need to see what's going on.*

She got a thumbs-up and huffy-faced emoji, likely for hanging up on her. *Fair.*

Before she could decide what to do, the cop car zoomed off.

"Oh come on," she muttered, getting out of her Bronco. That was when she realized Nick was striding toward her, holding up her license and insurance. Okay then, she thought the guy had left with her stuff.

"I didn't think it was possible for you to take a bad picture," he said as he held out her license.

"Hey!"

"I'm just kidding."

"No you're not." Her picture was hideous, but that wasn't important. "What the hell happened?"

"Oh, that was my cousin. My younger cousin, whose older brothers work for me. At first he was happy to see me, until he realized you and I work together. Said he got a tip that someone matching your description—the '69 Bronco, not you specifically—was transporting drugs."

"What!"

"This has got to be part of whatever is going on. Also...let's check your Bronco."

She glanced up and down the quiet road, her stomach tightening. She'd barely eaten all day and was starting to feel weak.

"Hey, come here." He took her off guard by pulling her into a gentle hug.

And god help her, she leaned into him as a wave of emotions threatened to drown her. "I feel like I'm living in a nightmare."

He made a soothing sound as he ran his big hand down her back in a gentle motion. "We're going to figure this out."

"I don't know how to deal with this nice version of you," she blurted into his chest.

"Yeah," was all he said on a sigh, but he didn't stop rubbing her back.

And thankfully he didn't pull away or act impatient as she got her emotions under control. He felt so good in her arms, all hard, warm and strong. And he smelled better than a man had a right to, like bergamot and something she couldn't put her finger on. But he smelled like fancy tea and… Okay, she was starting to spiral. And she was probably gripping him too tight, but she couldn't find it in her to care. Once she could breathe again without feeling that pull of fear, she stepped away and wiped away the errant tears. "Thank you and sorry," she muttered.

"Don't apologize. You're dealing with something no one should have to." Sighing, he stepped to the rear of her Bronco with her.

After unlatching the tire, she swung the bar open, then pulled up the window and unlatched the tailgate. The person who'd restored it had made some changes to make it easier to open and for that she was grateful.

Her hands trembled as she opened things up.

"No back seat?"

"I took it out, but still have it. I transport a lot of stuff in here." Her voice shook and she hated that. Hated whoever was doing this to her.

"Here. I know you can search, but let me handle this." His voice was somehow soothing but also commanding.

And right about now, she'd take it. Because she couldn't believe she was actually searching her vehicle for drugs. Even in her wildest days, she'd never been into anything like that.

He got to work, opening up her roadside kit, and before he'd said anything, she read his body language. Then he cursed.

"What did you find?"

"Don't touch anything," he said as he opened the black and red emergency kit a little wider.

She stared at the large packet of pills wrapped in cellophane. She didn't know what kind of drugs it was, but a bunch of pills wasn't a good thing. "I was expecting cocaine or something."

"Me too." Sighing, he stood back for a moment, then said, "Let's go directly to the police station."

"No way."

He held up a palm, and with the sun setting behind him, the man looked like an angel. A dark, avenging one ready to rip out someone's throat. That was way hotter than it should be. "Hear me out. You need to get on the record that someone is harassing you. This is the best way to do it."

"And just tell them that someone planted drugs in my car?"

"I'm going to handle that part."

"Nick—"

"Just trust me. And call Sinead, tell her we're on the way. She can meet us there."

She wanted to argue, but knew he was right. Because what if this happened again? She needed something on record showing that someone was harassing her, trying to set her up. If anything, if she did end up arrested in the future, this would help her demonstrate reasonable doubt of her guilt.

She hated that she was even thinking in those terms, but she had to be smart—smarter than whoever was coming after her.

Because screw them. More than being scared, she was beyond pissed. Whoever was messing with her had messed with the wrong Knight.

Chapter 17

As THEY ALL SAT in the sheriff's office, Berkley couldn't believe Nick was flat-out lying to the detectives. It was clear they weren't happy to be having this conversation here, so at least that was a plus.

Because apparently Sinead Goode was friends with the sheriff. Their families went way back—Krystal had told her, but Berkley would have figured it out considering where they were currently sitting.

"So you saw someone messing with the back of Ms. Knight's Bronco?" Detective Dewey's tone held more than a little disbelief.

"Like I said already, yes." Nick's tone was just this side of condescending.

"And you just...did nothing?"

Nick shrugged, the picture of nonchalance. "What the hell was I supposed to do? I pulled up to the jobsite, saw someone in a hoodie at the back of her vehicle. They heard or saw me arrive, I'm not sure which, then literally ran. I couldn't see any damage to her Bronco and figured they were looking to steal her spare or something." He paused, eyeing the other man. "Are you suggesting that I should have run after them?"

"No one is suggesting that." This from Detective Levitz, who had a much better poker face than his partner Dewey. That man just looked angry all the time now.

Maybe because he didn't have a slam dunk with Henry's murder?

In the last ten minutes, Berkley was starting to think Levitz was in charge of this investigation, not Santa Claus's twin.

Levitz looked at her now, his expression a lot nicer than it had been on Monday. Jeez, had all that only happened on Monday? "We're glad you came to us with this. We're going to process the pills and see if we can figure out where they came from. Now…" He looked at Sinead, then back at Berkley. "You said you had some information about Mr. Moore's murder?"

Berkley was really glad they were in a cushy office having this conversation and not the sterile, cold interrogation room, but she was still scared they were going to cuff her after she told the truth.

Most of the truth.

"We do," Sinead answered. "And I want it on the record that we came here of our own accord. My client is here because she wants to help find not only Mr. Moore's killer, but also figure out who has been stalking her."

Detective Dewey made a scoffing sound and Berkley's gut tightened even more. Maybe this had been a mistake after all.

"Got something in your throat?" Nick practically growled.

"Why are you even in here, Mr. Storm?" the detective demanded.

"I literally just gave an official statement about the harassment Ms. Knight has been receiving. We can leave right now if you'd like." He took a step toward Dewey that was clearly menacing, and oh, she really liked the way he said *we*.

Levitz cleared his throat, his focus now on Berkley. "Tell us what you know."

"Monday morning I woke up with a raging headache in a house not my own. I had no idea what was going on, or how I'd gotten there, just that I was in my pajamas in someone else's laundry room."

Levitz frowned, clearly not knowing where she was going with this. Because how would he? How would anyone guess this?

"Okay," he said slowly.

"I didn't realize it at the time. Not right away, anyway," she lied. "That I was at Henry's house."

The other detective cursed, but everyone ignored him.

So she continued. "My neck hurt and I suspected someone had drugged me. I was too out of it, and now I also realize that I was in shock. I woke up in a strange place, having gone to bed in my own house..." Swallowing hard, she shook her head, trying to play up the fear she'd felt.

And it wasn't hard, because the whole situation was terrifying.

"I thought... Well, I thought there was a chance I'd been raped or who knows what. So I ran."

"You...ran?" Levitz asked.

"Yes. When I realized I was in my ex's laundry room, I knew I wouldn't have gone there voluntarily. And without getting into the details of our relationship...I was scared." She felt Nick's gaze on her and had to ignore him.

"Where did you go?" Levitz's voice was calm, reassuring.

She still didn't trust him, but it made this easier. "I ran to my brother's house. He lives close to Henry. And like I said, I was in shock, moving on autopilot, I guess. I didn't know about the cops or Henry's...murder, at the time. Just that I'd been kidnapped. Or abducted, whatever."

"Why didn't you call the cops?" Levitz watched her carefully.

She couldn't hide the snort. "I didn't have my phone. I didn't have *anything* on me and I know for a fact that Henry donates a decent amount to the Fallen Officer's Fund. Not to mention I got into some trouble when I was young and dumb. Also...a friend of mine was raped and it was handled poorly by the cops." Also true, just something she hadn't thought of at the time, but she needed to sell this. "To put it simply, I don't trust you guys. I didn't trust any of you to handle with care what could have been an assault on me. My brother took me straight to the hospital where a friend of his ran a drug panel on me."

"Did they do a rape test?" Levitz's voice had softened even more, so maybe he wasn't a total piece of shit like his partner.

"No. I'd planned to but…I realized I still had my tampon in from the night before. And I felt…fine." She hadn't been sore anywhere and it felt weird to explain anything else with the room so full.

He nodded, encouraging her to go on.

Sinead stepped forward and handed him a file—the report from her drug test. "As you can see, she was drugged with a serious cocktail, including ketamine. Injected into her neck. And," she added, handing over another printout," these are the details from my client's security system. Someone turned off her system in the early hours of Monday morning. About an hour before she woke up in Mr. Moore's laundry room."

Levitz glanced over the printouts. "What about your camera system?"

"I don't know. It's a basic one I bought online. It sends me alerts if anyone triggers them, but…there's nothing on them in that time frame." Which bothered her, but she wasn't sure what to make of it. It was possible she'd turned the cameras off when drugged, but…there was just a big blank in her memory.

"Are you a heavy sleeper?" Levitz asked.

"Not usually, but I took a melatonin Sunday night because I needed the sleep." And she was cursing herself for that now.

Because she'd been dead to the world and someone had broken into her place, disarmed her system, then injected her with enough drugs to make her either compliant enough to leave on her own or knocked her out so she could be transported. *Twice.*

Levitz was quiet for a long few moments as he scanned the papers. Then he looked up at her again. "And someone broke into your place Monday night. Or attempted to," he added. It wasn't a question. "Do you have any enemies?"

Dewey made a derisive grunt. "Oh come on, you can't actually—"

Levitz glanced over his shoulder at Dewey, and though she couldn't see his expression, his voice was hard. "You don't need to be in here."

Unless this was some weird good cop, bad cop role, something was going on between them. She didn't think they were role-playing though.

Dewey clenched his jaw and was quiet, though he didn't make a move to leave. *Ugh.* She wished he would. His presence was making her feel off-kilter.

"Enemies? No. I can't think of anyone who hates me enough to drug me, dump me at Henry's place after he'd been murdered—likely by them—and plant drugs in my vehicle then call in a tip about it. That's psycho-level shit."

Levitz gave her a ghost of a smile. "It is indeed." Then he frowned again. "And it's very concerning, especially since someone spoofed those emails to your ex. It's clear that someone wants to hurt you. Where are you staying right now?"

"My brother's place. It's very secure and he's vigilant about security in general."

"You're not staying at your sister's?"

"No. Normally I would, but she's got kids and...I honestly thought it might be like a conflict of interest."

Levitz nodded slowly, his expression still unreadable. "I think it would be a good idea to put an officer on your house, at least for a few days. See if someone shows back up. But if I'm being honest, whoever is targeting you knows a lot about you. Enough to know your security code."

She'd already figured that much out. But they talked for a few more minutes until finally the two detectives left the office.

She let out a long breath, feeling as if she'd just come off a hard workout.

"I think it's safe to say you're in the clear for Mr. Moore's murder but...please be careful in general. Clearly someone wants to hurt you and I don't trust these guys to figure out who. Maybe Levitz," Sinead added a little grudgingly. "He's got a solid track record."

"Oh. That's good to know."

She nodded. "He moved up here from Atlanta. Has a high closure rate."

"And I won't be in trouble for telling them about waking up at Henry's after the fact?"

"No DA with any brains would bring a case against you for how you reacted. If they do, it's going to make the department look incompetent and...you're good. You didn't commit a crime by running. I can almost promise this is going to die. They've got bigger fish to fry anyway. A well-known doctor has been murdered and…" She lowered her voice even as she went to close the office door they'd left open. "There might be a connection to another murder. Same M.O." She looked at Nick. "I think you talked to them about the guy. James Reed?"

Berkley had to school her expression since she hadn't told her lawyer about waking up at Reed's place either. And it was waaaaay too late to tell the cops about that now. She'd be taking that to her grave. Micah had already assured her that she wasn't on any cameras at Reed's place so she'd be telling no one. It would just muddy the waters.

There was no need to tell them anyway. Especially if, as it sounded, the cops knew there was a connection. She'd planned to sneakily tell Krystal there was a possible connection but now she might not need to.

Nick nodded. "Yeah, I knew him just through work."

"He had some contact with one of my part-time workers," Berkley said because it would be weird not to bring it up and then have them find out later. Both turned to look at her in surprise and she hoped she kept her expression neutral enough as she shrugged. "I already told my sister this. She's investigating his murder. I didn't know there was a connection to Henry though."

Sinead watched her for a long moment. "They were both killed with the same type of weapon, same method. You don't know him at all?"

"No. I mean, his name only, but I never talked to him or anything. He called my business about cleaning out a condo development he'd recently bought." She shrugged, really striving for casual.

Sinead simply frowned, but then told her to "stay safe" again before she left, a faint cloud of Black Opium by Yves Saint Laurent remaining in her wake. She recognized the scent because Silvia also wore it.

And speaking of, she really needed to tell Silvia and Kendall what was going on. They were all close, and if someone was targeting her, there was no reason to think they'd stop at hurting her friends or family.

Even though she knew she was walking a fine line of lies and omissions, she just couldn't tell her friends everything.

Chapter 18

Nick slid into the front seat of his truck, shut the door.

"You totally lied about seeing someone messing with my Bronco." Already strapped in, Berkley sounded maybe not shocked, but surprised. And pleased.

Now that they were safely in his truck with no chance of being overheard by the cops or detectives, Nick lifted a shoulder. "I told you I had a plan."

"I didn't think that involved *you* lying to the detectives."

"Whoever is targeting you isn't playing by the rules, so we're not either." She just stared at him. "What?"

"I just always assumed you were like this...Boy Scout."

"I'll break every rule to protect people I care about." And she fell into that category, no way around it now. He'd been so wrong about her—and a giant asshole on top of it for making assumptions based on her ex-husband. His sister was right about him, and he was making things right, starting with Berkley.

Though that wasn't the only thing he wanted from her. He liked her at the most basic level. She was funny, kind. And fine, gorgeous. But there was a genuine warmth to her that he found himself drawn to, wanting to orbit around. To keep safe.

She blinked at him, looked as if she might say something but then turned away, her cheeks flushing pink as she strapped in.

Part of him wanted to push her a little, but knew now wasn't the time. Especially if he wanted to convince her to stay at his place. And by *convince*, he meant *bribe*. "So. You're staying with me. Not Apollo." Okay, he'd meant to be a whole lot smoother than that.

"What?"

He nodded. "Arlo is going to bring your Bronco to my place." They'd left her keys with the front desk at the sheriff's office and Arlo was only five minutes out.

"I think I must need to repeat myself, because *what*?"

"I talked to Apollo—"

"What? When?"

"When you were talking to the guy at the front desk. He's got a work emergency and my place is more than secure. And I've got a triple garage so your Bronco won't be outside where anyone can mess with it. Sure, it's drugs today, but what if someone cuts your brake line tomorrow? It just makes more sense." When she didn't say anything, he glanced at her and found her furiously texting.

After a few minutes of clearly angry texts—no doubt with Apollo—she set her phone down and took a deep breath. "While I greatly appreciate you and Apollo going behind my back, as if I don't have any agency—"

"I only found out ten minutes ago."

"I will be making my own living arrangements. I'll just stay at Micah's."

"Does he have a garage?"

She clenched her jaw but didn't respond.

So he decided to push it. Just a little. "I also have a part-time chef who drops off meals four times a week."

She still didn't say anything, but he saw a little more interest in those startling green eyes.

"Okay, I have something that might change your mind." As he pulled up to a stoplight, he unlocked his cell and handed it to her with a picture of Sunshine, the most adorable golden retriever who ever lived. Sunshine was even smiling at the camera, as if she knew her cuteness was being captured. She probably did.

"Who is this cutie?" Berkley's voice was softer now, and beyond excited.

"Sunshine. She's four years old, loves tummy rubs and evening walks."

"You fight dirty," she grumbled, but pulled her phone back out and sent a few more texts.

He did when something mattered to him. Or someone. "I take it...you're staying with me?"

"Oh no. I'm staying with Sunshine." Berkley sniffed slightly, but he didn't miss her smile as she looked out his truck window.

Chapter 19

"I NEVER WANT TO leave you," Berkley whispered to Sunshine, who was currently lying on a giant throw pillow next to her, just smiling at her as they lounged in front of the crackling fire.

Nick's place was impressive, even if it hurt to admit. He hadn't been kidding about it being secure.

His place wasn't in the country exactly, but it was on the outskirts of Sanctuary Falls in a neighborhood where each home sat on a three-acre spread. And since he had a ridiculous amount of cameras set up (he'd shown her) there was no way anyone was getting close to his house without being seen. His place was set back from the street with a privacy hedge, and just like he'd said, he had a three-car garage. He'd left out that he also had a gorgeous sparkling, *heated* pool. She wouldn't be getting in it tonight, but this was the kind of place made for entertaining.

He was currently putting something in the oven for dinner—he hadn't been kidding about having someone cook for him. She could get used to that.

As she continued rubbing Sunshine's belly, she called Silvia.

"Um, who is that sweet girl in the picture you just sent?"

Oh yeah, she might have texted selfies of her and Sunshine to everyone she knew. She needed to lay the groundwork for when she kidnapped this good girl. Dog-napped? Because Nick who? Sunshine had *always* been hers.

"My new dog."

"What!"

"I'm kidding. Mostly. Sunshine is Nick's golden retriever. You know, if I don't *kidnap* her." She raised her voice, hoping it would carry from the living room to the kitchen where she could hear him moving around.

"Oh my god, I'll help you. She's soooo cute and fluffy I want to bury my face in her fur."

"Get in line," she said on a laugh before recapping to Silvia everything that had happened.

"Holy shit, B. That's...not good. And yeah, I know that's an understatement, but wow."

"I know. It's a lot to handle."

"My number one suspect would be Henry but he's..." Silvia cleared her throat. "Anyway, maybe it's, I don't know, one of the nurses he slept with?"

"That's a thought... But why would they do this to me?"

"Yeah. I don't know. I'm just trying to imagine *anyone* who would want to hurt you like this and I literally can't come up with someone that makes sense. *Maybe* an ex-boyfriend from long ago, but why now?"

"I thought about that too." She had one ex in particular who'd been a born loser. And that wasn't something she said lightly. But everything he touched turned to shit. She also hadn't had anything to do with said loser in nine long years. It would make no sense for him to come after her now. Also, she couldn't see him having any patience to drug her and move her to a different location. Or the brains to plant drugs in her vehicle and call in a tip.

No, he'd be more likely to smash in her windows or something equally destructive.

"I hate that I'm heading out of town... You know what, I can cancel my trip. You should be staying with me, not Nick Storm."

"No. Thank you, but no. Seriously. I'm actually glad you're leaving town. It means that whoever is trying to hurt me can't go after you. How long are you gone anyway?"

"Ah, only a couple days, but I don't like the thought of—"

"The detectives have things under control. They're actually trying to find the real killer now instead of focusing on me. And you're one of my closest friends, something that's not a secret. Everyone knows I love you and Kendall. It's better if you're gone for a while."

"I...hate that you're right. Are you sure you're okay at Nick's house? I mean, after the way he's been with you?"

"Yeah." She lowered her voice. "He's been a lot different than I expected. I think he's trying to atone or something for being a jerk."

Silvia snorted.

"What?"

"Nothing. Just...be smart."

"Always. Oh, if you get hold of Kendall before me, will you fill her in on everything? I've been calling her but she's not responding. And this is too much to text."

"I will. She's been working doubles though and you know how they are with their new cell phone rule."

Yeah, she did. They were sticklers about the nurses leaving their cell phones in their lockers. Which was bullshit, but also not her problem. "I'll text her a brief outline just to let her know to be safe."

"Good. She's smart about walking to her car with a buddy."

"I know." It still didn't make Berkley feel that much better. Not when some faceless lunatic was out there wanting to hurt her. The next step would be to target people she loved. At least her brothers were all badasses and her sister was the scariest of them all.

By the time they got off the phone, Nick had stepped into the living room, looking gorgeous in the casual clothes he'd changed into. His hair was also still a little damp and he had no shoes on. Seeing him in his home, his element, so relaxed was...making her see him as human.

Which of course he was, but everything about the last few days was a lot to handle. And having Nick treating her so differently, protecting her, was the most shocking of all.

"If you're hungry, everything's ready. Or I can bring you food while you lounge with Sunshine." He raised an eyebrow, looking at the two of them in amusement.

"What do you think, girl?" she asked Sunshine.

Who licked her face in response.

"For the record, I don't recommend eating on the rug next to her—she's shameless and will try to steal your food."

"It's not stealing if I give it to her, but you're probably right." As she got to her feet, her phone rang again, this time her sister. "I need to take this really quick."

He nodded and headed back into the kitchen where she had the perfect view of him walking away—with the perfect ass—and being all domestic.

Watching him move around in the kitchen was way sexier than it should have been. And the fact that he'd lied to the cops for her today... She was pretty sure she was falling for him without meaning to.

Chapter 20

SIGHING AS SHE READ Peter's text, Krystal sent him back a thumbs-up. She hated working these ridiculous hours but had no choice now. They had to wrap up Reed's murder case, especially since it now seemed it might be linked to Henry Moore's. Asshole that he'd been, he still deserved justice.

She was surprised her boss hadn't taken her off the Reed murder since there might be a connection to Henry, but apparently the sheriff didn't think there was a conflict of interest now that her sister wasn't a suspect anymore.

Well, she was pretty sure that dumbass Dewey still thought Berkley was guilty, but he was the worst in so many ways. She couldn't wait until he did everyone a favor and retired.

She headed into the kitchen, found all three of her boys sitting at the island top, and paused for a moment. She loved seeing them like this. Relatively quiet, eating together, just happy and safe. Having them all under the same roof settled something in her.

"Hey boys."

Jett looked up from his food and phone and grinned. "Hey Mom. We promise to clean up when we're done."

"I know. I just wanted to let you know I have to run out."

"Is this about Aunt Berkley? Is she okay?" River piped in.

"It's not about her, but yes, she's okay."

"She should just stay with us," River grumbled.

Krystal had already had that argument with her sister, and lost. "I promise she's safe where she is. I literally just got off the phone with her."

"Is she still mad at us?" Miles asked, pushing his now empty plate away, his quesadilla demolished.

"She was never mad at you guys." A conversation she'd had with them multiple times since her birthday. "And for the record, you're never this upset when I'm mad at you." She kissed the top of Miles's head and got a groan, but he didn't pull away at least.

"You just said she wasn't mad."

"Fine, she was disappointed."

River and Jett groaned.

"In case I'm not back in time, please make sure you're in bed by nine and brush your teeth." Nine really meant nine thirty and sometimes ten, but as long as they got eight hours of sleep, she figured she was doing all right.

They all agreed with grunts and she knew her window of communication with them was over for now. They were much chattier when it was actually bedtime. Or when she was driving them places.

When she couldn't find Mike in his office she started calling him, but found him in the garage as she headed out. "Oh, hey," she said on a laugh as she slid her phone into her purse. "Peter just texted. We're following up on something, but I shouldn't be home too late. Hoping to be back by ten."

Mike's body language was off as he held up what turned out to be the prom photo she'd stolen from Myron's office. "What the hell is this?"

"Ah, not sure about your tone, but it's a prom picture." What was his deal? He'd never been jealous and definitely not about her high school boyfriend.

"I see that. Why was it in your SUV?"

"Because I stole it from Myron a couple nights ago."

"You were at his place?"

"At his bar, yeah, for the Reed murder. He's not so much a suspect as a source at this point. Why were you in my work vehicle?"

"I wanted to do something nice for you and clean it out."

That was when she saw the bag of trash he'd clearly just filled up and the mini vacuum. "Oh, thank you. That's really sweet." And unexpected, if she was being honest. Not for the "old Mike" as she'd started thinking of him, but the last six months had been...kinda shitty. She'd been ignoring it mostly but knew they needed to talk about whatever was going on in their marriage.

"You didn't think to tell me that you saw your ex-boyfriend and...what, had dinner with him? Or something else?"

"Oh my god, you can't be serious." Something inside her snapped because this was bullshit. "First of all, if you're implying I'd ever cheat, you're out of your mind. Second, when's the last time you actually asked me about my day?" Oh crap, she was shouting now. The boys were inside and wouldn't be able to hear them in the garage so she didn't hold back.

She couldn't. She swore it was like something had broken in the last few months and she couldn't keep her emotions buried any longer.

He started to respond, but she cut him off. "You don't have to answer because I already know. Six months ago you stopped giving a shit about anything other than your new job. And I understand wanting to succeed at something, but not at the cost of our relationship. The only thing you ever ask for is 'Have you seen my pants' or 'Where is Jett's permission slip' or a dozen other similar questions. But as far as asking about my day or my life or me in general, you stopped. And to be fair, after four months of asking you about your job and what's going on in your life and getting absolutely nothing, I stopped too. Because it hurt too much to keep begging for something from you and get nothing in return. Do you even remember the last time we had sex? It was still bathing suit season!"

Adrenaline pounding, she vomited all the things she'd been holding in for months.

He just stood there staring at her, and oh my god, she loved him so damn much but she just couldn't look at his handsome face one more moment.

Because six months was a long damn time for no sex, especially for the two of them. Add on the other stuff… She wanted to puke.

Because deep down she'd been worried he was cheating on her, and now as he just stared at her in shock, she wasn't going to risk him blurting out some version of that.

Nope.

If he was cheating, he could tell her later. Because she had a murder to solve. She slapped her palm against the garage door button, then got into her vehicle and left. She was very intentional not to peel out of there when all she wanted to do was burn rubber.

Chapter 21

Micah stepped into The Laughing Llama, owned by Louis Cain. A piece of shit Micah wanted nothing to do with, but he had to go where the leads took him. At least the name of his bar was funny.

With Berkley safe at Nick Storm's house, he could breathe easier. He'd been combing over James Reed's records and the man had not only owed Myron Booker money, but Louis Cain as well.

And Cain wasn't someone you wanted to owe money to. He took any bet, but he was also suspected of running a drug hub right out of his bar. Micah didn't think the pills were distributed here, but from what he'd heard, they sure took in the cash here.

If someone was looking for a payday—and didn't mind going up against armed men—this would be the type of place to knock off.

To his surprise, he spotted two familiar faces inside the smoky bar—yep, this shithole still allowed smoking indoors. At least they seemed to have decent ventilation, but he hated the insistent smell. Instead of getting his own table, he headed straight for the booth Krystal was sitting at.

She raised her eyebrows at him. "Come here often?"

"You couldn't pay me enough. I think we might be here for the same reasons."

She gave him a ghost of a smile. "Somehow I doubt that."

He hated lying to Krystal more than anyone, so he was going to give some half-truths. Leaning forward, he said. "I'm following a lead about James Reed's murder."

His sister went very still.

Yep, he shouldn't know shit about Reed since Krystal had no idea of Berkley's connection to the dead man. But he needed to know what the detectives knew. "Word is that Henry and Reed were killed in a similar manner. I already have a lot of info on the *cheating bastard*," their loving nickname for Henry, "but I started digging into Reed to see if I could find a connection."

"What, why?"

He just stared at her. "Come on." Like he wasn't going to try to figure out who was after Berkley.

She huffed out a sigh but paused as a server with a surly expression approached their booth. The woman was in her twenties, had an "eat shit and die" expression to go with her black and white T-shirt that said *fuck you* in binary code.

He laughed at her shirt, which earned a small smile. Or at least less rage as she set her hand on her hip. Her manicure showcased glossy black nails. "What do you want?"

Leaning back, he turned on the charm his sisters swore he had. "Surprise me."

She quirked an eyebrow. "Surprise you?"

"Sure. I love it when a woman orders me around."

The woman glanced at Krystal, frowned, then looked back at him with more rage. "You're flirting with me in front of your—"

"I'm his older sister," Krystal murmured, her tone dry.

"Oh." He got an almost smile now. "You might regret letting me choose."

"I doubt it. If your tastes are as good as your shirt, I trust you."

"You're the only person in this dump who's ever gotten what it means."

He grinned at her, and even with the eye roll, her cheeks flushed pink as she stalked away. She wasn't his type, but he wanted information and would work the flirting angle if it got him intel.

"She might put eyedrops in your drink."

"Nah. She likes me, I can tell."

Laughing lightly, Krystal shook her head. "It's your damn face."

"My face?"

"You've got that boyish charm and you know it."

He grinned even wider. "I *do* know it. I just wanted to hear you say it." Unfortunately for him it did nothing for the woman he was slowly becoming obsessed with. She was immune to his charm.

His sister's expression dimmed a moment later. "Why are you looking into Reed?"

"If there's a connection to Reed and Henry, I want to know."

"Peter and I have this covered."

"Yeah, I saw him when I walked in. He looks too much like a cop, so hopefully you came in separately."

She nodded. "About half an hour apart. Hey, I *know* how to do my job. And don't try to distract me."

"Fine. Worth a shot..." He cleared his throat. "Look, Reed had a gambling problem."

"I *know*."

"I figured you'd already talked to Myron, but Reed owed a lot more to Cain." He murmured the last part low enough she might not have even been able to hear him. But she read his lips clearly enough because she nodded.

"There's no way he'll talk to me. I was hoping to find something here to give me cause for a warrant. See if I can get him in interrogation."

"I can help you with that."

She was already shaking her head before he'd finished. "No. No gray area stuff."

"Fine, be that way." He paused as their server approached with a bright orange drink.

In a hurricane glass with a lime and strawberry garnish to go with the little blue umbrella, the drink got a few sidelong glances. People mostly ordered beers or whiskey in this place.

But he took it with a smile. "Hurricane?"

"Yep."

"Thanks."

She looked faintly surprised as he sipped on it, but then grinned and shook her head. "That one's on me, you weirdo. You guys hungry?"

It looked as if Krystal was going to say no but he beat her to it and ordered a couple deep-fried appetizers.

When they were alone again, he said, "I'm setting something up for a job. Nothing to do with Berkley. It will help my cover if I become a semi-regular here."

Krystal watched him carefully. "Do I want to know the details?"

"Probably not, but I'm killing two birds with one stone right now. Because to be clear, I *am* trying to find out who the hell targeted our sister." And if he got a name before Krystal did, that person was dead. He'd already talked with Cormac and Apollo. Whoever wanted to hurt their sister wouldn't see the inside of a jail cell if they got to them first. Their body would never be found.

"Fine. Can you share what you've discovered about Reed so far?" she asked.

Because his sister might be a rule follower, but she wasn't going to turn down good information even if she knew he'd likely gotten it illegally.

Or creatively, as he liked to say. "Of course." And while they were talking, he covertly took pictures of multiple known felons with connections to illegal drugs, among other things.

Each one headed down the hallway that led to Cain's office at one point during the evening.

Oh yeah, he was definitely running his money out of here. Or at least collecting payments.

That was his first mistake. This place was too open, too public. Cain should have been more careful.

Chapter 22

"Hey, what are you doing here? Not that I'm not happy to see you," Berkley added as she finished cleaning out and organizing one of the bedrooms. She'd made incredible time with this particular bedroom and had tagged what she thought the Storm siblings might want to keep, donate or definitely sell.

Clover looked around the room, her eyes wide. "I can't believe all you've done."

"Bessie Carmine might have been a pack rat, but she had a weirdly good organization system."

Clover strolled around the room, looking at the different Post-it notes. "I like that you've color coded everything."

"It'll make our lives a lot easier later. And I'd planned to call you this evening anyway to let you know in case you wanted to start looking at some of this stuff. I can work on getting the keep and donation items where they need to be. It'll really clear out this space for when we have the estate sale and get the auction website up." The estate sale stuff would be a different beast and she usually waited to set up their sale link once they were closer to the end of the cleanout.

"Oh, sure that sounds good." Clover looked as if she wasn't paying attention as she ran her hands over an antique French settee.

"Is everything okay? Did my brother do something stupid? Also, are you guys dating? I've been wanting to ask and now I guess I'm just doing it." Maybe she shouldn't have, but whatever. She was nosy. And Micah had been weirdly quiet about things too. Normally she got more details than she wanted from him. But every time she called or texted he said he was "busy running down leads."

Clover looked at her in surprise, then groaned. "Am I that obvious?"

"No. I mean...I can tell something is up, but you told your brother about me getting hauled into the sheriff's station. It wasn't hard to figure out that you and my brother are like, hooking up."

"Oh, we're not dating. Or sleeping together." Clover looked almost horrified that she would think that. "Not that Micah's gross or anything," she added.

Berkley laughed as Clover stumbled over her words. She held up her palms. "I wouldn't care or judge if you were."

"I know. But we're not like...together or anything. He's just...helping me with something and he's being annoyingly obtuse about some of the things he's doing behind the scenes."

"Ahh. That's a Knight family problem." Also, she was pretty sure that Micah was into Clover, whether the woman was into him or not. But yeah, he wasn't good at sharing things so she could see that being a problem if he really was helping Clover with something.

"What is?"

"The 'I'm doing this for your own good' and 'don't worry your pretty little head about it.' My brothers are obnoxious like that."

Clover grinned. "My brother is pretty obnoxious too."

Yeah, but he had grown on Berkley. So much that she couldn't stop thinking about him...or a better word would be obsessing. "But he loves you."

"True. Though we have been sort of arguing."

"Really? About...this job?" There had clearly been some miscommunication between the two of them and she was curious how it had worked out. Obviously okay since the contract had gone forward, but there had to be more to it.

"Sort of. But also just him being a dumbass," she said dryly.

Which made Berkley smile. "I'm done for the day... Want to do something fun?"

"Ah yeah, should we let Arlo know?"

"Oh, we're not going to leave the house." No way. She was taking her safety seriously. And that meant staying put until Nick got here to take her back to his place. She might not love the restrictions, but she did love being alive. So there was that.

"What do you have in mind?"

Berkley grinned. "This way."

Chapter 23

Beyond exhausted, Nick stepped into the kitchen to find Arlo boxing up different sets of antique-looking drinking glasses. "Everything good?"

"Yeah."

"You get roped into work?"

"It's actually interesting and I hate just sitting around."

Yeah, he'd known that, and it was part of the reason he'd hired Arlo for Berkley's security. He wasn't just going to sit on his ass and do nothing all day. But it was a quieter job than the man was used to. "If you want me to rotate you out early, I can ask one of the other guys to keep an eye on things here the next couple days." Nick would be taking over as soon as he finished up contract negotiations on a job that would be a game changer for his company. He wanted to be the one watching Berkley.

"Nah. I'm not complaining either. I like Berkley. And she really knows her stuff. I offered to do this and promised not to break anything with my 'big meaty bear paws.'"

He blinked. "She called your hands big meaty bear paws?"

"Not her, Clover did—and it wasn't a compliment." Arlo chuckled as he continued packaging one of the flute-shaped glasses. "And I don't think she was being ugly to me. I think she's angry at the male population in general. At least that's the vibe I was getting." He shrugged, then added, "I've got three sisters. I know the signs. Someone's pissed her off and I know it wasn't me." He gave Nick a pointed look.

Nick just cleared his throat. "Ah. Well keep up the good work, then. I think I'll just need you through the end of the week, but I'll take over on Monday."

"I'm fine either way. I've learned a lot more about twenties-era stemware today than I ever could have imagined, so there's that. Oh, they're in the front parlor room by the way."

Nick stepped into the formal parlor near the front of the house and stared. The room was a lot for the eyes to take in. A massive floral rug covered most of the original hardwood floors, and peacock-themed wallpaper added to the rich riot of color. Then there were the purple velvet couches, thick green velvet blackout curtains with gold braids holding them back to let light in, oversized art with people in various states of undress, a few Grecian busts, and so much color everywhere it felt like pure chaos. He liked the actual architecture, but the decor was just too much.

By the window, in two jaguar-themed sitting chairs that had to be modern, Clover and Berkley sat wearing fur coats and drinking something that looked a lot like champagne out of dark yellow, vintage champagne glasses.

"What...are you guys doing?" He glanced between the two of them, then paused as they both dissolved into laughter.

"Talking about our *wonderful* brothers," Clover said, her tone saying the exact opposite.

"Ah, so talking trash about us, then?"

Berkley focused on her drink, but snort-laughed before taking another sip. God, even her laugh was adorable.

"I plead the Fifth. Also, I'm keeping these glasses! And maybe this coat." Clover stood and twirled around in it.

"It looks good on you."

"Of course it does." She sniffed slightly, then turned back to Berkley. "Thank you for this afternoon. I needed this. I'll call you later?"

"Definitely." Berkley stood and pulled her into a hug, murmured something that Nick couldn't hear before his sister strode out of the room—while giving him the side-eye.

They hadn't talked much since her big blowup and he wasn't sure how to reconnect with her. He knew he had to make the first move but he wasn't sure what to say. Other than to apologize again.

"We didn't drink any of the real champagne from the collection here, just sparking grape juice," Berkley said as she picked up the empty glasses.

"I wouldn't have cared if you had drunk the real stuff. Clover is part owner too."

Berkley didn't respond, just made a *hmm* sound.

He followed her to the kitchen and took the glasses when she went to wash them. He started handwashing them instead. "So how was today?"

"Very productive. But I can't keep my mind off everything. Someone wants to hurt me, send me to jail, if not outright kill me, and... I don't know. It's just a lot of not knowing. Not having a face to put to the threat. But more than scaring me, I'm now just really, *really* angry." She slid the fur coat off and set it on the back of one of the kitchen chairs. "I called Levitz today and he wouldn't tell me anything. Though he was pretty polite, unlike his jerk partner...and I'm rambling, aren't I?"

"No. I want to hear about your day. I called Levitz too and he gave me the runaround as well, if it makes you feel better."

"You called?"

"You don't have to sound so shocked." Instead of setting the glasses on the drying rack he started hand drying them because they clearly went with the set Arlo had been packaging up.

She winced. "To be fair, you were sort of a jerk to me anytime I saw you for the last year."

"I wasn't a..." He trailed off as that instinct to defend himself kicked in. He wanted to be better and being honest was the way to start. "I wasn't the best."

She snorted in agreement as she picked up a roll of packing tape to seal one of the already labeled boxes. "So...Henry told you I cheated on him and you believed it, huh?"

He'd already told her as much but apparently they were actually going to talk about it. Which was probably a good thing. "He was very believable."

She let out a startled laugh. "Yes, he was."

"He hurt you." A statement, not a fact.

She eyed him for a long moment, the tape still in her hand. "He did. Not physically. That would have actually made it easy to leave. Maybe he knew that, I honestly don't know. One of his exes came to me after the divorce, told me he used to slap her. Literally slap her face when he was mad. Never took it further, she said, as if that made it better. And I believed her. I think he would have gotten worse eventually though. That stuff always escalates."

"Jesus." Nick leaned against the countertop, shoved his hands in his pockets. "I never would have guessed. The man healed people. *Helped* them. He'd saved Clover's life. Not an excuse... or maybe it is. But I trusted him because he saved her."

She was silent for a long moment, but finally spoke. "Men like him—or people, I guess, but it sure seems to be a lot of men—wear very good masks. And yes, he was skilled at his job—and he had the god complex to go with it. Obviously I wouldn't have married him if he'd shown me who he really was. I blamed myself for a long time for marrying him. As if I should have seen something he was *actively* hiding from me." She made a scoffing sound. "My sister called me out, asked me if I realized how dumb that sounded. And when she put it in those terms it was easy to see. He hid who he was, so of course I didn't realize how awful he was. He didn't want me to know."

"I'm sorry you went through that." And a very dark part of Nick wanted to ram his fist into Henry's face and not stop. But the guy was dead. So.

"Thank you. When I found out he was cheating on me—on an industrial level apparently—it was so easy to leave. And I hated myself for needing that excuse, I guess. A reason that people would understand. Because leaving a

man like Henry, who people worship..." She shook her head. "In the beginning, he love-bombed me, something I see clearly now. I actually realized it
about a year into our marriage when his façade started to crack."

"You left though, and that's brave."

"Yeah, maybe. I'm still mad at myself for not leaving sooner. Because I
should have. I just thought... If I stayed, if I was, I don't know, better, that he
would change. And then when it was clear that I was seeing the real him, the
person he'd hidden from me, I should have left. But I had been known as the
screw-up Knight. Or the wild one, whatever. I didn't want to fail at something
else, have everyone think, I don't know...that silly Berkley screwed up again.
'Look at her, she married the kind, successful doctor and couldn't even make
that work.'"

He shoved out a breath, hating the pain buried in her voice. And that he'd
believed the lies without getting her side of the story. "Is it wrong that I'm not
sorry he's dead?" He surprised himself by actually saying what he was feeling
out loud, but the words were out there now.

She blinked, then let out a sort of horrified-sounding laugh. "I'm not sorry
either," she mock-whispered. "He was awful in so many ways. Ways that I'm
still learning about covertly from people."

He could only imagine. Henry Moore had been a master manipulator.
"Clover told me that he hit on her during one of her check-ups."

Berkley rolled her eyes. "I'm so not surprised. He hit on my friends too. The
man... You know what, screw him. I'm done talking about him, but thank you
for listening."

He nodded. "I'm just sorry I judged you wrongly. That I judged you at all.
My sister has recently pointed out to me that I have a history of doing that
and I'm trying to be better." He *wanted* to be better. For Berkley, but mostly
for himself. He hated that he was carrying around so much shit from his
childhood.

She lifted a shoulder. "We all judge things, usually based on childhood
trauma."

He raised his eyebrows, wondering if he'd said that last part out loud. Or maybe she'd just read his mind.

"Oh, I'm in therapy," she said. "But seriously, so much of the shit we carry with us into adulthood is crap from our childhoods, even if we don't realize we're still carrying it." Another shrug. "And on that note, want to get the hell out of here and get some dinner?"

"I would love that." He wanted more than just dinner with her.

He found himself wondering if once this nightmare was over—and it was going to be over soon, he swore it—if he and Berkley had a shot at something real.

Because his feelings for her were growing every second he spent with her. And every second he was apart from her. Didn't seem to matter if he wasn't around her; she was all he could think about.

Chapter 24

"Thank you for another incredible dinner." Berkley leaned back in her seat at Nick's kitchen table.

Sunshine was sitting in between them, eyeing both of them carefully as if she was watching a tennis match—and hoping for them to drop something edible. Berkley might have snuck her a few green beans, which she'd devoured with relish.

"I wish I could take any of the credit."

"Well you heated it up in the oven so that counts for something." The enchiladas topped with extra layers of cheese and sour cream had been the perfect end to the day. She wasn't above using comfort food to make herself feel better.

"True. I'll take the credit, then," he said with a laugh. "Should I leave some out for your friend?"

"Even though I want to say no and hoard it all to myself, yes," she said on a laugh. "And thank you again for letting her come over." Kendall was finally getting off a long run of back-to-back shifts so she, Berkley and Silvia—who would be joining them via video—would get to talk about everything going on.

"Of course," he rumbled in that deep voice she was becoming obsessed with.

Or maybe she just *was* obsessed. Not becoming. Hmmm.

He continued, interrupting her wayward thoughts. "I'm sure you've already talked to him, but I spoke to Micah earlier today. He said he's been monitoring your security cameras and system and your house has been quiet."

She was surprised he'd been in contact with Micah, but quietly pleased that he'd been looking into things. Since barreling his way into the interrogation room with Sinead, she'd seen a different side of Nick. She'd never had anyone other than her siblings be so protective of her. Though this was very different. "Yeah, he told me that, but I think he's keeping something back from me... You said you knew James Reed, right?" She tried to keep the question casual-sounding.

"Yeah. Sort of. He hired my company to do a gut and reno job that could have turned into something big. Why?"

"Just...the M.O. of his murder and Henry's were the same apparently. But it doesn't seem as if he and Henry knew each other. Or if there is a connection, the cops don't have one yet. Well, that they've told me," she said dryly. She wasn't sure her sister would tell her anyway. Krystal just wanted her locked down and safe.

"Reed had a gambling problem though, right?" he asked as he made a plate for Kendall.

"Yeah." She bit her bottom lip as she debated telling him more. Because sitting on it was making her crazy. So far he'd proven that he would go out of his way to protect her. Hell, he was keeping her safe in his well-secured home. Something that was incredibly hot. A man who wanted to keep her safe and cook for her? Yes, please. Apparently that was her weak spot. "I need to tell you something," she blurted.

He paused what he was doing, those gunmetal gray eyes finding hers as he leaned against the countertop. "I'm listening."

Being under that kind of intense focus was unnerving, especially since it was coming from Nick, a man she'd imagined naked more times than she wanted to admit. But she managed to make her voice work. "You know how I woke up at Henry's in my pajamas after being drugged?" Of course he knew.

"Yeah." He sort of drew the word out as he nodded.

"Something similar happened to me at James Reed's house," she whispered. "I woke up fully dressed in a stranger's kitchen. Someone had hit me in the back of the head—it's actually still a little sore. Anyway, I called…someone. They picked me up and helped me retrace my steps from the night before." She recapped most of what had happened, leaving out the mention of Micah because she wasn't sure it was necessary. It probably wasn't even necessary to tell him any of this, but in her gut she knew she could trust him. Sure, it was terrifying to open herself up like this, but he'd been proving who he was over and over the last few days. She was going with her instinct.

He stared at her for a long moment after she finished, let out a slow breath as he pushed up from the countertop. "Jesus, Berkley."

She tried not to focus on the way his forearms flexed when he moved. "I know, it's a lot."

"No, not that. Someone is clearly targeting you. We already knew that, but this adds a new element. When their first attempt didn't work, they tried again, this time with drugs. And they took you straight from your house. That's an escalation… We need to share this with Sinead's investigator."

She knew the woman named Luna had found out that her email had been spoofed, but Berkley doubted she was looking into things any further now that Berkley wasn't a suspect.

"I *can't* tell the cops about my connection to Reed. I don't have an alibi for when he was murdered. I might…have even been at the house, unconscious at the time. I could have actually been at his place at the time of the murder. I only found out later from Krystal that there was so much forensics at the house it was as if someone dumped random DNA everywhere. She normally doesn't talk about her cases, but I overheard her on the phone to her partner. They can't figure out why there was so much DNA there."

Nick frowned. "We can find out if it's the same deal at Henry's murder scene. Or Sinead can."

"Exactly how tight is she with the sheriff?"

"Not her, but her father. And if she plays Levitz right, she can probably convince him to share information if he thinks her investigator will share what she's found. I only say this because she's shared Luna's information before with the department and it's been useful, so she has a solid track record."

"But we leave me out of everything?"

"Definitely." He gave her a long look. "You must have been so scared when you woke up."

"I was." Still was, if she was being honest. Right about now she wanted to step into his arms and let him comfort her in more ways than one.

He looked a little murdery, though she knew that wasn't directed at her as he said, "This changes things on another level. The connection...it feels personal. Someone dumped you at these two places, then when you didn't get arrested for murder, they try to set you up for running drugs."

"I know." The knowledge sat heavy in her gut too. She wrapped her arms around herself, wished it was him holding her. Even as she told herself it was ridiculous to crave his touch, she knew it wasn't. This man had gotten under her skin.

"You sure you can't tell Krystal?" He took another step toward her, his expression softening.

"No." She shook her head sharply. "No way. Not unless it's absolutely necessary. She needs plausible deniability. And it'll look really bad if I come out now and say something. I don't want to put her in a position where she has to lie for me. I hurt my sister enough when I was younger. I'm not doing it now." She just couldn't. Krystal had been only twenty when their mom had been murdered and she'd stepped up, taken over everything while their father ran off and drank himself to death.

He nodded, looked as if he was going to say more, but his doorbell rang, a gentle chime echoing through his big house. He glanced at his phone, likely looking at the camera system app. "Your friend is a little early." He almost sounded disappointed and she wondered if he'd been thinking along the same lines as her.

"That's a first," she murmured with a light laugh. "I'll go let her in."

"And I'll make myself scarce. I know I said it, but treat my place like yours."

"Thank you." Those two words felt so inadequate but it was all she had.

As she went to answer the door, she hated that she wished Kendall was already gone because she wanted more alone time with Nick. She didn't think it was her imagination that something had sparked to life between them.

The timing might be stupid, but she found it hard to care when she was sharing a roof with the man doing everything he could to keep her safe.

***

Lounging on the bed in the guest room Nick had given Berkley, she and Kendall were talking to Silvia via Berkley's tablet. Sunshine had wandered off, likely to cuddle with her owner. Something Berkley wished she was doing herself.

Shaking off that thought, she smiled at Silvia through the screen. Even though she wished Silvia was with them in person, she was still glad the three of them could finally get together and talk.

"How's your current investigation going?" Silvia usually looked into cheating spouses and even had a funny Insta page for all her exploits (with faces blurred out and real names changed).

"Good enough." But there was something Silvia was holding back. Normally she loved to talk about work shenanigans. "I want to hear more on what Kendall was going to say about work though. What's this big gossip?"

Kendall shot Berkley a glance she couldn't read.

"What? Is it about Henry? Whatever it is, you can say it." The man had been murdered, of course he was a topic at the hospital. It only made sense. And Berkley wanted to know everything she could about what people were saying.

Kendall nodded as she let out a breath. "I wasn't sure if I should but...there's a lot going on, so buckle in. First, there's a group of nurses who think you killed Henry. Are convinced you somehow masterminded it." She rolled her eyes.

Berkley tried to shove down the instantaneous burst of nausea. People actually thought she'd killed him? She'd been staying off social media and throwing herself into work because it focused her. But of course people would be talking shit. Sanctuary Falls had a small-town feel but it was more medium-sized. And yeah, she could see that rumor taking off, especially if they'd been under Henry's spell and believed his lies about her.

Great, more shit for her to worry about.

"What a crock of shit," Silvia muttered.

"I know. And I've been calling it out. But that's not the real tea. Henry was screwing this nurse—Ada—and I know this sounds crazy," she said, lowering her voice. "But I swear I saw her stealing drugs. As in a giant bag of them. Pills mostly, but also supplies."

"Wait, what?"

"Yep. And I've heard from two techs that they caught her in places she shouldn't have been."

"Have you reported her?" Silvia asked.

"I want to, but she and I got into it a few weeks ago and I feel like it'll come off as me trying to get back at her. And it's just my word against hers."

"Do you think Henry knew she was stealing?" Berkley asked, wondering about this new angle, especially since the woman had taken pills. She made a mental note to tell Levitz or at least her sister the woman's name so they could follow up with her. If she was the one who'd planted those drugs in Berkley's car, it stood to reason she'd done even worse.

"Maybe, but I doubt they talked much, if you know what I mean," Kendall muttered.

Berkley nodded but filed the information away. "Someone needs to tell the detective on his case about this. Or at least tell him who Henry was dating."

"Oh, that hot detective has been to the hospital a few times. He's interviewed a *bunch* of people who worked with Henry, including Ada. Henry was sleeping with a doctor though too, another surgeon. I assume the detectives know about his extracurricular activities."

"Which doctor?"

"Sophia York."

"Oooh, I remember her," Berkley said, her stomach tightening. "She was awful to me any time I stopped by the hospital."

Kendall nodded. "I'm not surprised. She and her husband are going through a nasty divorce right now. I have no idea if it's because of her and Henry or if she started screwing him after they broke up."

"I swear the hospital is wilder than a soap opera," Berkley muttered.

"You're telling me."

"You guys..." There was something in Silvia's tone that had both of them straightening.

"What is it?" Berkley asked.

"I'm not supposed to talk about this, but the investigation I'm working on has nothing to do with cheating spouses. An insurance company hired me to look into a pending case against the hospital." At Kendall's surprised gasp, Silvia held up a hand. "I couldn't talk to you about it before and I probably shouldn't be talking about it at all now. But in the course of my investigation, I stumbled across something else."

"Ooh, what?" Kendall sat up straighter.

"I can't say. Not yet. But if you find out about more drugs going missing or get actual proof, will you let me know? I'm talking names of *anyone* involved."

"Definitely." Kendall grinned. "We need to start our own podcast."

"Not this again," Berkley groaned as she fell back on her pillow with a laugh. Even with the heaviness of everything going on, being with her friends eased that tension.

Though there was another kind of tension coiled inside her, one she was pretty sure only the man down the hallway could take care of.

Chapter 25

Make sure Levitz talks to Ada Dator, a nurse at the hospital. K told me she had a thing with Henry and is suspected to be stealing pills. Might be worth looking into.

Parked in her garage, Krystal read Berkley's latest text, saw more dots appear, then disappear. So whatever she'd been about to say, she decided against it.

Krystal texted her back, then shot off another one to Levitz and Peter. At this point, Levitz was working with them and not against them. She didn't bother to include Dewey because he was useless. She got immediate responses from both men so that was good.

You're sure you're good at Storm's place? She texted her sister one more time because she couldn't help herself.

OMG, I'm good. Thank you for checking but please don't worry about me. Then a picture of a massive pool came through, followed with a selfie of Berkley and a golden retriever named Sunshine, who was also, weirdly, smiling too. So her sister actually *was* good and not just faking it.

Seeing Berkley smiling so goofily even with all this going on warmed Krystal's big-sister heart. She was always going to worry about her siblings. That was simply the way it was. Their mom had been murdered, something that was still hard to think about since it had never been solved. And their dad, useless man that he'd been, had abandoned all of them so it had been up to her to take charge. Luckily she'd had Apollo helping out that first year but then he'd joined the military...and she was just wasting time in her head instead of going inside.

Her sister was safe at the moment and that was what mattered. She just needed to figure out how Henry's and James Reed's murders were linked.

At least she was close to getting a warrant on Cain's bar. She'd gotten enough overtime approved for one of their younger officers to hang out at the bar today and they'd gotten a lot of pictures similar to the ones she, Peter and Micah had taken, with known felons moving in and out of the back of the bar.

But more than that, they'd gotten pictures of the bartender serving two underage girls and a couple other petty crimes. Which meant they had enough for a warrant. She had no idea if Cain had murdered Reed or was even involved, but Reed had owed Cain money, and the only way to get someone like Cain to talk was to force him. Because he wouldn't make a statement on anything if he didn't have to.

And since they couldn't even find a cell phone bill linked to Cain, they couldn't track who he talked to. The man operated as a ghost, likely using burners. She still couldn't figure how he'd be linked to Henry but the pills were coming from somewhere. The hospital was a likely spot to be funneling pills. Though it was hard to imagine that prick Henry doing something like that.

And she was officially done for the day. She needed to eat, shower and sleep. Or just sleep.

Exhausted before she'd even walked in the house, she tried to mentally prepare herself to see Mike. He'd texted her an hour ago asking if they could sit down and talk.

The optimistic part of her hoped this was a good thing. Before the past six months, they'd had no problem communicating. Things hadn't been perfect, but they'd been pretty damn good. And she'd looked forward to going home, unlike now.

Steeling herself, she stepped into the kitchen and paused. Blinked.

Looked around.

Countertops were clean, no dishes in the sink, dishwasher running. And the biggest thing of all—or maybe second biggest—there was a candle lit on the island top. And she realized that wasn't a big thing, but her husband had *cleaned* cleaned. Not some half-ass bullshit. Everything was sparkling.

And the biggest thing she noticed, there was a pot of...yep, chili on the stove. It was simmering and smelled amazing. Two bowls were set out along with a bag of Fritos and shredded cheese.

Okay, so maybe tonight wasn't going to suck.

"Hey." Mike stepped into the kitchen, his hair damp, expression tentative.

"Hey. You cooked." *Wow, way to state the obvious.*

He gave her that boyish grin she'd fallen for long ago and she felt her heart do that little flip she'd forgotten about. "Yeah, I'm pretty overdue."

"We both are." They'd been living off takeout and that wasn't good for any of them. They'd lost all their structure over the last six months, something she had to take partial responsibility for.

"You hungry?"

"Starving." She hadn't thought she was when she was sitting in the garage, all tense and worried, but something had loosened inside her now.

"I'll make you a bowl...but first, I'm sorry for being such a shit. No excuses, just sorry," he blurted, standing by the stovetop, looking lost.

She shoved her hands in her jeans mostly so she wouldn't cross the distance between them and hug him. Because that's what she wanted to do. She missed his arms around her, the way they used to fall asleep holding each other.

"Have you cheated on me?" She needed the answer. That was the one thing she wouldn't forgive. Well, she wouldn't forgive other things, but this was the only thing weighing on her.

His eyes widened in surprise. "The fact that you're sincerely asking means I haven't been doing a good job as a husband. Something I already know. And no," he added. "I could never. There's no one for me but you. And I know I acted like an asshole about that picture. I *know* there's nothing between you and that cocky prick."

She snorted. "Nothing but annoyance."

"On your end. He still wants you."

She shrugged and stepped closer to Mike. "Probably true, but I only want you." Since practically the moment they'd met.

He shoved out a sigh and covered the rest of the distance between them, pulling her into his arms. "I've got some stuff to tell you. Stuff that's going to make you mad. But I know we can work through it."

"I'm not loving where this is headed," she said against his chest as she hugged him back. As long as he hadn't cheated, they could work through whatever was happening. "So dish me some chili and let's talk."

He stepped away to grab their food, and while she was tempted to open a bottle of wine, she was worried she might get called back in to work. "You want a beer or anything?"

"Water is good. Jett reminded me to 'hydrate' as he left today."

She let out a startled laugh. "That sounds exactly like him. 'Mom, you're drinking too much caffeine!' As if that child knows what too much means."

"He's not wrong."

"I know." She loved all three of her boys equally but Jett had a covert caretaker's soul. He was always looking out for all of them in little ways. "Where are the kids anyway?" She'd known they weren't here since it had been so quiet.

"Playing basketball with the Jensen kids."

Good, that meant they'd be out for a couple hours. "So, what's this stuff that's going to make me mad?"

Sighing, he set the bowl in front of her before sitting across from her. "There's no good way to say it. I took half my retirement account and invested it in the startup. It's why I've been working around the clock the last six months."

Um. What. The. Hell. She blinked, beyond surprised he'd done something so stupid, and without even discussing it with her first. But she also knew she couldn't say that if they wanted to have a productive conversation.

"Say something. Yell at me."

"No... I don't know what to say. That was...a choice." *A really stupid choice.* Also something she couldn't say—or shout, because that wasn't going to be productive.

"It was insane, I know. But we're already in the black." She saw a glint in his eyes she hadn't seen in months. He was excited about this. After leaving his old tech company, he'd broken off with some coworkers to start their own, and she could admit she wasn't a hundred percent sure what they did. It involved a lot of math, statistics and a bunch of stuff that made her eyes glaze over. But her man was smart with that kind of stuff in a way she could just scratch the surface of.

"That's good."

"It's incredible. We didn't think we'd make a profit until at least the two-year mark but things...look good." There was that glint again, a little brighter.

"From that look I'm guessing better than good?"

"If things keep on the same trajectory, I'll be able to re-fund my retirement account over the next few years to get it back to where it was."

"You'll have lost all the interest."

He held up his palms, his chili still untouched. "I know, but it was worth it."

"Why didn't you just tell me, then? Not ask me, because at the end of the day, it is your account. Technically," she added. "Because our retirement accounts affect *both* our futures." And it hurt that he hadn't run such a huge financial decision past her. It wasn't like him. If anything, he usually over explained things to her.

"I...don't know. I was scared. Not of you, just scared, I guess, to take this chance. I didn't want any outside noise—and I'm not calling you noise—"

"You kind of are," she murmured.

"Fine. I wanted to do it and I didn't want to have a discussion about it or the possibility that you'd say no. I was thinking that I'd do it and ask for forgiveness later. And I know that's messed up. I was selfish and ended up throwing myself into the programming so much that the guys finally told me I was going to burn out."

Yeah, she could have told him that. "You've had no work-life balance. No work-*family* balance," she added.

"I know. I already talked to the boys. Game nights are back on and there are going to be some changes around here."

"Yeah?" She dug into her chili, her stomach still twisted up, but at least they were talking. She hated that he hadn't come to her, wasn't sure how long it would take her to process that. She could forgive him, but it didn't take away the hurt. Or the damage to her trust. They'd always been honest with each other. Maybe too honest.

"Yep. I've made a chore schedule for the boys. And if you're on board, I want to hire a bi-weekly cleaner. You and I are working our asses off right now, and while the kids will be doing some stuff, they've got school and sports."

"They need to just be kids some days," she murmured.

"Exactly. I know we talked about hiring a cleaner before, but you didn't love the idea."

She mostly hated the idea of a stranger in her house. "I'm actually open to it. As long as I get to vet them."

"Of course. So...on a scale of one to ten, how mad are you? Before you answer I'd like to make it clear that the rest of the house looks as good as the kitchen and I plan on going down on you later tonight until you come. Hopefully more than once."

She laughed at the deadpan way he said it, knowing he wasn't joking. And her stomach was doing flips again. "I'm not mad, just disappointed and hurt. Honestly. We could have had a conversation and figured things out instead of having no communication and things just falling apart the last six months. Don't get me wrong, I could have spoken up sooner or... I don't know. I'm really just hurt. And you broke my trust in a way... This sucks." But she was still down to get naked later, which told her just how much she'd missed him.

"I wish you were mad. And I'm sorry that I hurt you. More than I can say."

She could hear the sincerity in his voice, see it in his expression. This was the man she'd married. The one who'd been open about everything. "Thank you."

"So...can I ask you about Berkley? And your case? Also, I think she's plotting my murder after that colossal screw-up."

Knowing that they had a ways to go to come back from all this, but still feeling lighter, she nodded. "She would never kill you, but only because you're the boys' father. And this case..." She shook her head. "Peter and I have followed up on so many leads. Reed, that's the vic, was a mostly stand-up guy from what we can tell. Or he was until recently. He got into some debt from gambling and owed money to the wrong kind of guys."

"Ah, so that's why you were at Myron's? And sorry, I have to ask—that dick had that picture up at his work?"

She smothered a smile, knowing he wouldn't appreciate that she was amused. Right now she was still pretty hurt, but she loved that he cared. "He did."

"I want to wipe that smug look off his face every time I see him." He spooned more of his chili, looking a little murderous.

Which she shouldn't find so hot. "And how often do you see him?"

Mike paused. "Fine, fair. But twice a year is enough for me."

She just shook her head. "We're trying to follow the money, essentially, with Reed's murder. But we're going around in circles."

"And Berkley really woke up at Henry's place? I know you're not on that case but you hinted there was a connection?"

"The style of murder was almost exactly the same. Whoever stabbed them was precise and struck right in the same place. That kind of kill takes skill, meaning that it's likely not the first. Or even the second. Whoever did it is a killer. And the amount of DNA at both crime scenes is ridiculous. It's like someone went through a bunch of garbage cans, found random shit, and then sprinkled it all over their houses. It's mostly nail clippings, hair, but there are other fibers too."

"You do love a mystery."

"Not when it could involve Berkley. God, she looked so scared at the station. I wanted to pummel Dewey for talking to her without a lawyer."

"Another asshole I'd like to throat-punch."

She snickered. "Get in line." Sighing, she sat back. "I've missed this, missed talking to you."

"Me too. I didn't realize how bad it was until about a month ago. Then I didn't know how to fix it, and I kept telling myself I would talk to you. Then I'd get sucked back into a coding problem and..." He reached across the table, took her hand in his bigger one. "I never want to lose you. I know how lucky I am to have you and our boys."

"Same," she whispered. "And we're going to be okay." She felt it in her bones. They just had to start talking again. Start acting like a damn family that actually liked each other.

He started to respond but her phone rang, Peter's familiar ringtone.

She sighed. Peter never called after hours unless it meant they had to go back to the station or follow up on something that couldn't wait.

But thankfully Mike just grinned. "I'll make you a fresh pot of coffee and pack a to-go thermos."

That tight band around her chest loosened again as she slid off her stool and rounded the table to hug him hard. "Thank you."

He hugged her back. Hard, and kissed the top of her head. "I'll throw in the brownies I made too. Tell Peter not to eat them all."

She laughed as she leaned back up to look at him. "I might not share at all. And I love you."

"I love you too... Also, I planned a spa weekend for the two of us a month from now at that place you love in Wilmington. Already talked to Apollo. He's going to stay with the boys. I'll text you the dates so you can ask for them off. It's a make up for messing up your birthday."

That stupid instinct was on the tip of her tongue to tell him it was all right, but it wasn't. And she was glad he was doing something to make up for it.

They really would be okay, she knew it.

But she sighed again when her phone started ringing another round. "Yeah, yeah," she muttered to Peter who couldn't hear her. Hopefully they'd finally gotten a break.

Chapter 26

BERKLEY MOVED QUIETLY THROUGH the house, glad Nick had enough dim lighting that she could see well enough without having to turn on overhead lights.

Unable to sleep, she was hoping to find a good snack in his fridge and maybe a glass of wine. Instead, as she stepped into the darkened kitchen she found Nick standing in front of the open refrigerator—shirtless.

The light did a perfect job of illuminating his washboard *everything*. Abs, pecs, biceps, holy hell, the man was *built* built. She'd kinda figured (okay fantasized about it too) since he worked in construction and his shirts and pullovers could only hide so much, but damn.

"Ah...sorry," she whispered, then wondered why she was whispering. "I couldn't sleep."

"Me neither," he murmured with a smile. "And I'm not hungry either," he added as he shut the fridge. "But please feel free to raid it."

"Work stuff keeping you up?" she asked instead of opening his fridge. There was recessed lighting above the cabinets, throwing the kitchen into a soft, warm glow. One might even say *romantic*. Not her, but someone might. She sat at the island countertop. "Also, do you have any white wine?"

"Not work stuff," he said as he pulled out a glass for her, then yep, he did indeed have an unopened bottle of pinot grigio. "Just going around in circles about what you told me."

"It's a lot." She turned at a soft *click, click, click* sound, smiled when Sunshine trotted into the kitchen.

The golden retriever made a sort of snuffling sound as she stared at the two of them and stomped her paw once.

"Is she annoyed with us?" Berkley asked, because Sunshine was throwing them major side-eye.

As if in response, Sunshine snuffled again, stomped her paw again, then turned around, swishing her big fluffy tail before she disappeared back into the hallway.

"She likes her beauty sleep." His tone was dry as he popped the cork. "And she gets annoyed if I don't go to bed by ten. No, I'm not kidding. So yeah, she hates it when I get up and interrupt her precious sleep."

Berkley snickered. "I love how big her personality is."

"I do too." There was unmistakable fondness in his tone. "And to go back to your earlier question... I don't like how personal those attacks on you feel, and I hate that I can't do anything about it."

"I know. I really do. I hate feeling so useless. Part of me wants to investigate things myself but...I don't even know how I'd do that. I guess I could ask Silvia for help but she's got her own stuff going on." A job she couldn't even give them full details on. "And it just feels dangerous when I know the detectives are working on the case."

"I agree," he muttered, leaning against the countertop.

It took all of her self-control not to drink in every hard line of the man, to not allow her gaze to dip lower, lower... So she focused on her glass. Not the half-naked, way too sexy for his own good man who was keeping her safe at his house.

And watching her through heavy-lidded eyes.

Oh, she was not mistaking that look. Was she? Feeling more than out of sorts, she took another sip of her wine and realized she'd almost drunk all of it.

Yep, it was time to go to bed. Or at least get some space from Nick Storm and those soul-searching eyes. She slid off the stool and went to place the glass in the sink. "I think I'm going to head back to bed." And you know, proceed *not* to get any sleep at all. Maybe she could try counting to a billion and see how that worked.

As she stepped back from the sink, a strong, callused hand grasped hers.

Instead of making a quick escape, she turned into him, inhaled that intoxicating masculine scent. Before she could blink, however, he just took over, slanting his mouth over hers in a heated claiming she felt all the way to her toes.

She could think of nothing but the feel of his chest under her fingertips. The staccato rhythm of his heartbeat as he teased his tongue against hers, as she teased him right back. He might seem like he was in control on the outside, but he was just as affected as her.

He was barely touching her, simply cupping the back of her head in a possessive grip, but that was all she needed. Because she was on fire for him in a way she'd never experienced.

This man who'd made everything inside her light up the first time they'd met. Even when he'd pissed her off, when she'd wanted to wipe that smug look off his face, she'd also wanted to sit on his face to do it.

Because oh my god, his other hand was sliding down her body now, clutching onto her hip. There was something about the possessiveness in his hold that sent even more ribbons of heat curling through her.

When he suddenly pulled back, breathing hard, his face so close to hers she wanted to trace her fingers over his cheekbones, all she could do was stare. Apparently anything else was outside her skill set at the moment.

"Is this okay? I'm not pressuring you—"

Oh my god! She grabbed his face, and yep, he took the hint and kissed her right back, pressing her up against the island top.

Now it was all skin to skin, not just a hand on her hip and her head. Nope, she was getting to feel all his powerful body against hers as he nipped her bottom lip with his teeth.

She moaned into his mouth, feeling impatient and desperate for more. It was probably stupid to hook up with him when she was stuck under his roof for who knew how long, but she absolutely didn't care.

Worrying about the after of this was a problem for future Berkley.

Slowly, sensually, he slid his hands up her hips and started teasing the hem of her pajama top.

"Is this okay?"

"Yes." God, did she sound desperate? Whatever, she wasn't sure she even cared. "And for the record," she rasped against his mouth, "it's okay if you take off the rest of my clothes too. You don't have to ask."

The slow, wicked grin he gave her before brushing his mouth over hers again, whew, it sent another heat wave through her. This man was going to do wonderful things to her body and she wasn't going to have any regrets.

Nope.

Tomorrow was a new day, and right now she was going to take life by the balls and enjoy it. Someone wanted to hurt her, was out there plotting against her. Well screw them.

But first she was screwing Nick Storm.

After he stripped off her top, she leaned into him, savoring the way her nipples brushed against his chest. Sucked in a breath at the sensation of being so intimate with him.

So vulnerable.

Weirdly enough, she didn't feel vulnerable, but empowered. He'd done nothing but try to keep her safe, literally keeping her out of jail since barreling into her life less than a week ago. This man was safe, something her body knew even if she was starting to get up in her head again.

When he slid her bottoms—and panties—off, her brain took another break and she spread her legs in invitation. Thinking was definitely overrated.

He growled against her mouth, an actual growl, before he hoisted her up onto the countertop. "I've been fantasizing about going down on you since the coffee shop." It sounded like a confession.

One she was happy to hear. Her inner walls clenched, heat rushing between her legs at his words.

Keeping his gaze pinned on hers as he slid one of his big hands up her thigh, waaaay too slowly for her liking, she felt as if he could see straight through to her soul.

And when he slid a finger inside her, she gasped, unable to stop the response even if she wanted to.

"You're so wet."

She wasn't sure why, but his words turned her on even more. She rolled her hips, silently begging for more. Because right now she was walking a tightrope of control, not sure that she even cared if she lost it. "More." That was all she could get out.

Thankfully he was in control and more than happy to give her what she wanted.

With another kiss, he crouched down between her spread thighs, urging her to lie back as he began teasing her with that wicked, wicked tongue.

He made her feel like nothing but her pleasure mattered, that they were the only two people who existed as he slid another finger between her slick folds.

It didn't take him long to find that perfect rhythm, his fingers thrusting in and out of her as he focused on her clit with the patience of a man who knew what he was doing.

"Nick." She slid her fingers through his hair as he sucked on her clit, the action taking her off guard in the best way possible.

Her hips rolled off the countertop at the sudden jolt of pleasure and she felt that ripple go through her entire body. She was so damn close, and she might have told him just that, but she couldn't be sure she got the words out.

When he increased his rhythm and focused solely on her clit, she forgot everything else until she was coming against his face and around his thick fingers. Her orgasm hit her so fast and so hard she finally had to stop him from teasing her when the pleasure bordered on pain.

Splayed out on his countertop, she'd never felt so satisfied in her life—and wondered what that said about her previous sex life.

Suddenly he was there, leaning down over her and tugging her up to him as she spread her legs to accommodate his size.

"I love the sounds you make when you come," he murmured before kissing her in another raw claiming where she tasted her own pleasure.

"Now I want to hear you come." She bit his bottom lip as she slid her palm down over his very hard reaction to her. His lounge pants did nothing to hide his reaction, and feeling how much she affected him sent another rush of power through her.

She absolutely loved that this was all because of her.

She squeezed him once, grinning at the way he shuddered under her touch. He rolled his hips into her hold, still kissing her as she slid her hand down the front of his pants.

He was thick and hard and she loved the feel of him in her hands.

She might have no idea where they went from here, but she wanted the chance to find out. Even if this didn't last, she'd never been so attracted to anyone, and oh god, he was moaning into her mouth as she gripped him harder, stroked him harder.

He clasped onto her hips, his fingers digging into her as she tightened her grip. "About to come," he rasped out.

She stroked him even faster, moaning with him as he came hard and long in her grip before resting his forehead against hers, his breathing raspy and uneven.

"That was incredible." He kissed her once then slid her off the countertop. "And we need to clean up."

She let out a startled laugh at his words, but didn't argue as he led her to the sink. She was coming to find out that he was really thoughtful in so many unexpected ways.

The picture she'd painted of him—which was mostly his fault—was so much different than the man she'd been getting to know. The one who was keeping her safe and the one who'd just brought her so much pleasure she was still reeling from it.

She didn't think she'd made a mistake tonight, but she was also pretty sure she'd just gotten in way over her head—because she'd definitely caught feelings.

Chapter 27

Nick stepped into his bedroom, realized that his shower was running.

Berkley was in *his* shower.

Which meant she was definitely naked.

His brain short-circuited for a moment as the image of her orgasming right on his countertop hit him hard. Then another image trickled in: her curled up in his bed, still naked. She'd tried to return to the guest room last night but he'd been having none of that.

So he'd hauled her to his room and she hadn't complained. Just fallen fast asleep.

Sunshine had sniffed at her face a few times, then gone back to her bed by the big window where she was currently curled up and basking in the warmth of the sun.

He'd been up for an hour, had let her out, fed her, made coffee, then come back to his room expecting Berkley to still be sleeping.

She could have gone back to the guest room while he'd been occupied and taken a shower in there, but she'd chosen to stay...

He didn't step inside even though the door was half open. It felt like an invitation, but he didn't want to make any assumptions right now.

After what they'd done in the kitchen last night, they'd talked about protection and since she was on the pill and they'd both been tested recently, they didn't need a condom. Something he was incredibly grateful for.

"You want company?" he called through the door opening.

"Company and coffee are welcome. But I can wait on the coffee."

He grinned at her tone and pushed the door open.

Anticipation was already building inside him as he stripped off his clothes in record time. Maybe he should be embarrassed by how desperate he was to be with her, but nope.

He was already aroused by the time he stepped into the expansive shower, but at the sight of her, he groaned.

Standing under the water stream, her dark hair plastered around her face and shoulders, she was his fantasy come to life. He'd loved every second of last night but hadn't been able to appreciate all of her like he could now.

There was more than enough natural light streaming in from the high windows. And right now she looked like a goddess with the sun highlighting her full breasts and all her curves and lines. She was petite, but with curves and he wanted to worship all of them.

When she slid a hand down her stomach, her intentions clear as she watched him, he took a step forward.

To his surprise, she laughed, the sound echoing in the enclosure.

"I was wondering what it would take to break that spell."

"I'm enjoying looking at you," he murmured, cupping her hips and pulling her close.

"Right back at you. But I'd like to touch you too." She traced her fingers up his chest, clearly enjoying the feel of him.

And he loved that she was as into this as him. Because he couldn't get enough of her. Part of him wondered if he was making a mistake by getting so invested so damn fast, but he'd kept people at bay most of his life. With her, he found that he wanted more. So much more. And he couldn't get that if he tried to put distance between them. Berkley was too full of life to settle for that. And she deserved someone who was all in.

Even if the thought terrified him.

Shutting down the voice in his head, he leaned down and claimed her mouth as she went up on her toes to meet him.

The little moan she let out as his erection brushed against her stomach had him even harder. In that moment he wished he had four hands because he wanted to touch her everywhere, to bring her so much pleasure she couldn't think straight.

Since he knew she loved it when he went down on her, if her reaction last night was any indication, he slowly, sensually kissed a path from her mouth, aaaalll the way between her legs.

She pressed her back against the wall and threw a leg over his shoulder, spreading herself perfectly for him.

At that moment the world felt like it shrank to just the two of them. There was no outside threat, just them. He held on to that as he slipped a finger inside her and began teasing her clit with his mouth.

The sounds she made would be forever etched into his mind, just as the way her entire body tightened as she raced closer and closer to release.

"I'm almost there." Her words were barely loud enough to hear over the rush of water.

But the way she dug her fingers into his head, urged him on, would have told him exactly how close she was.

He wanted to be inside her though, knew her climax would be that much better with him filling her, so he eased back.

She made a sound of protest but he stood fast, claimed her mouth as he cupped between her legs in a possessive grip.

"I want to be inside you when you come."

She leaned up on her toes again, nipped his bottom lip before she took him by surprise and turned around.

Oh hell.

When he realized what she wanted, he groaned and gripped her hip again as she placed her hands against the tile.

He'd planned to pin her back against the wall, but he liked this angle too, knew it would be deeper for her this way. By the time he thrust into her, he was almost ready to come.

Not quite, thanks to that last shred of control, but when she started pushing back against him, moving her body with his, he had to hold on to that control even tighter.

The way her body gripped him as he thrust into her was everything he'd fantasized about. But she still needed to come.

Slowing himself down, he reached around her body and palmed her clit, began that slow rhythm she seemed to like.

And when she started moving quicker against him, he increased his tempo until he felt her inner walls tightening faster and faster around him.

By the time she started coming, he was too, finding release in long, hard strokes as she cried out his name.

Even though he hated pulling out of her, he eased out and gathered her into his arms as she turned to face him.

"I really like showering together," she murmured against his chest, making him laugh.

"Me too." He could get used to it. Something that should scare him, but it did the opposite.

He wanted more of this. More of her. And not just temporarily.

But first, he needed to make sure she was safe. To end the threat to her for good.

Chapter 28

"Asshole Feds," Dewey growled for what felt like the twentieth time as six of them crowded into the observation room.

The interview with Cain was being recorded, but they were still utilizing the ability to watch in person without being seen.

Krystal ignored Dewey, but shared a sideways glance with Levitz, who wasn't as bad as she'd originally thought. Wasn't his fault he'd gotten a shit partner. At least Dewey was retiring soon.

Then she turned her attention back to the two-way mirror because things were finally starting to get interesting.

Louis Cain sat next to his lawyer, his expression defiant while his lawyer was the picture of calm. She was *almost* as good as Sinead Goode—an attorney Krystal only knew by reputation and was damn thankful her sister had retained—but not quite that killer level.

"If Torres is his attorney, Cain can't be as high up the food chain as we thought," she murmured to Peter, who nodded.

Levitz did as well, frowning in realization. "If he was really working with one of the cartels or East Coast families, he'd have one of the big hitters representing him right now."

"Yep. Which means..." She trailed off, not saying what they were all thinking—the Feds were going to try and cut a deal. They wanted a bigger fish, which meant they needed someone on the inside. Someone who would talk. Considering they had two agents in the observation room with them, she kept that to herself.

Krystal still wasn't sure if the Feds had taken over because of the similar murders or the suspected link to drug running through North Carolina and up the East Coast. She didn't think Cain had kidnapped her sister and dumped her at Henry's, or even murdered Henry, but...the Feds had much broader resources.

Something had made them roll into town late last night and take over both Henry's case and the Reed murder case. At least they were letting Krystal and the other three detectives watch the interrogation, along with two of their own people who might as well be clones. Dark suits, white shirts, black ties and boring as hell loafers—they looked like they were trying to mirror the Men in Black. If they were, kudos to them, because they'd nailed the look.

"We've already got you on running drugs directly out of your bar. Two of your people have flipped on you," Raine, one of the Feds said from across the interview table, looking at Cain and not his lawyer. "You've got quite the intricate operation."

Neither his lawyer nor Cain said anything, just waited. Clearly they were both used to this type of situation and were not going to talk just because a Fed said some of Cain's people had flipped.

"What we're interested in is who's behind these murders." Raine, a tall woman with jet-black hair was still talking while her partner stayed silent.

But her partner, an older man named Bush, started laying out photographs. From her vantage point she could see that the first picture was of Henry on a morgue slab. The second was of Reed. And oh, wait, the guy wasn't done. In all, he laid out eight images, all clearly dead men. Each of the victims looked to be white men in their thirties or forties, with dark hair. It was hard to tell for sure from where she was standing, but there were clear similarities at least.

"Wait, this is a serial killer thing? And you're just now telling us?" Dewey demanded, saying what they were all thinking. "Just like the Feds to roll in and steal the glory."

"Quiet," one of the Feds in the room snapped at him without turning toward the old detective.

Dewey stomped from the room, but Krystal was having the same thought. Moving around Levitz, she slid in next to the man who'd told Dewey to shush. Hell, she approved and wished Dewey knew how to read a room. "Is this actually a serial killer thing?" she asked quietly, hoping he wouldn't shut her down. The Feds had been pretty decent, all things considered.

He was silent for a moment, but nodded as the interrogation continued on the other side of the glass. "We think so. We've got eight so far but we think there might be more. But it's...complicated."

That didn't sound good. "How so?"

The man glanced at her, his dark eyes penetrating. "I know your sister was involved—"

"She didn't do shit."

"Not involved like that." He looked away again, his jaw clenched tight as she, Peter and Levitz waited for more. "I said we've got eight, but we think whoever killed Reed and Moore has killed at least ten. The complication is that two of those cases have been solved. Or more specifically, at least two people have been found guilty of the murders. They have the same type of story your sister did—they woke up in a dead person's home. But unlike your sister, they didn't run. They called the cops."

"And...took the fall."

"Maybe, maybe not. Maybe they're guilty after all, but..." He shrugged.

"What's the connection between the murdered people?"

"Mostly drugs or gambling adjacent. Henry Moore though...he's a little different. We don't have anything linking him to Cain or running drugs in general. But the M.O., the murder weapon, it's all the same."

"So...complicated."

"Yep."

She glanced back at Peter, who she swore could read her mind sometimes. No wonder the Feds had taken over.

He murmured something about grabbing a coffee but she knew he was going to try and get the file the Feds had, to find out the names of everyone who had been murdered in the same M.O. as Reed and Henry.

"You know we'll have to bring your sister in," the Fed said a few moments later.

Maybe she should learn his name. "Yeah, I figured."

"If you want to pick her up for us, make it easier, it's fine with us."

"If you think I'll bring her in without her lawyer—"

The man's mouth curved up ever so slightly. "I wouldn't dream of asking that. We think she might be able to shed some light on things. Or at least give a different perspective."

"You want me to pick her up now?" Clearly that was where this was going. The guy was opening up to her for a reason.

"Yes."

Holding back a sigh, she nodded. Whatever was going on, was a lot more complicated than they'd originally imagined.

She might not hate these Feds, but no way was she going to trust them with her sister's freedom.

Chapter 29

Berkley was still riding high, hours after this morning's fun in Nick's shower, as she pulled out another dusty box from one of the third-floor bedrooms of the Carmine Mansion. She'd never seen him coming. Literally or figuratively.

Never expected someone like him to walk into her life. They might have gotten off on the wrong foot, that being an understatement, but she really liked him.

And she could admit that it scared her. She'd had ridiculously poor taste in men when she was in her early twenties. Thought she'd made a better choice with Henry, and look how that had turned out.

Nick was different, but in a good way. She liked how driven he was with his job, how he talked to his sister on the phone, and weirdly, she loved the way he'd barged into her life and taken over.

She was used to being the "wild Knight," the screw-up who couldn't get her shit together. And sure, he'd been a jerk to her after listening to Henry's lies but...he'd apologized for it. And more than telling her, he was showing her who he was. She could forgive his first assumption about her. *Had* forgiven him.

Hell, the man had clearly paid for her lawyer, even if he hadn't specifically taken credit for it. She wanted to ask him about it, but things between them were... Well, she wasn't sure what they were.

They'd had sex. Really, really good sex. And she was staying with him until...the lunatic out there was caught. Who knew how long that would be? She hadn't thought that far ahead.

Part of her wanted to overanalyze what had happened between them and what would happen in the future, but she shelved all that and focused on separating the nineteen twenties hats from the random eighties ones that had been shoved into the storage box.

This place really was a gold mine of not only valuable items, but history. The owner had possessed an incredible eye, and if she'd had remotely enough money, Berkley would have bought this place herself.

Living in it was probably impractical since she was only one person, but whatever. She could dedicate rooms to different eras...

She paused at an incoming phone call, felt her heart rate kick up just at the sight of Nick's name. It was only ten o'clock so she was surprised to hear from him so soon.

"Hey, is everything okay?" she asked.

"Just wanted to hear your voice."

Oh, damn. Okay, she was clearly not prepared for him because her stomach did a little flip at his sweet words. Unlike with her ex, they didn't feel forced or fake, something she could only see now with hindsight. "Well hello, then," she said, feeling lighter. "I'm happy to hear your voice too. How's work?"

"Boring. Too long. And I'd rather be with you." There was a sexy growl to his tone that she felt all the way to her core.

"Is it weird that your whining is kinda hot?"

"Whining?"

She snickered.

"Have lunch with me?"

Normally she just ate on the job, and had been planning on taking a break around noon and doing just that. "You might be able to convince me."

"How about I eat you for lunch and then we try that Thai place on Iberia Street?"

She swore she could feel his smile through the phone and found herself smiling back. "I love that idea, but I hope you know if I start taking lunches off, I won't finish this job as quickly."

"Screw the job." Another growl.

She laughed. "Pick me up at twelve?"

"Make it eleven."

She smiled at the impatience in his tone. "Sounds good."

Even with the threat hanging over her, she felt safer when he was near so she would be counting down until eleven. Only an hour to go.

***

Berkley had been working for another half an hour when her phone buzzed with an incoming call. She paused at the unknown number that flashed on her screen. This was her personal cell, not her work number. Normally she ignored unknown numbers, but just in case it wasn't spam, she answered.

"Hello?"

"I have your friend.," a creepy robotic voice said. "And if you don't follow my instructions exactly, she dies. But it won't be a quick death. I'll cut her apart, piece by piece, starting with her pretty mouth."

Ice slicked down her spine but before she could respond, the call ended. "Oh god!" She started to call the number back but a barrage of texts flooded her phone, buzzing one after the other from the same unknown number.

She froze as pictures of Kendall came through. Tied up, one eye swollen, face bruised. Her friend was curled up on some kind of stone surface, her arms behind her back and her legs bound.

Oh god. Oh god, oh god, oh god.

She started to call Krystal but froze again as another text came through.

If you even think about calling the cops, or your sister, I slit her throat right now. But if you play along, you might get out of this alive.

Bullshit.

Still, she stopped herself from calling her sister and waited for more instructions.

If you want to save your friend, bring the lynx coat from the Carmine Mansion along with the three-carat diamond necklace.

She blinked. Wait, what? The coat and necklace were worth a lot, but this was insane. And how did they even know about them? And what did this have to do with Henry's murder? Or James Reed? What the hell was going on? Another text came in even as she tried to wrap her mind around whatever this was.

You will tell no one and leave your cell phone at the mansion. I have someone watching and I'll know if you deviate from your instructions.

Then the person sent coordinates and told her to be there within thirty minutes.

She plugged the address into her GPS and frowned. It was the falls she used to hike to when she was younger with...Kendall and Silvia. Oh god. Everyone in town hiked there in the summer. It was a hot spot, but in the dead of winter it was desolate, isolated. Everything was iced over and Kendall was curled up on some kind of rock formation.

She looked at the picture again. Now she knew exactly where this asshole was keeping her friend. The place was so isolated right now, but it didn't matter. Saving Kendall was the only thing she could focus on.

She was barely going to have enough time to get there.

She nearly jumped when another text came through.

If you leave now, you can make it on time. Leave your phone behind. I'll be tracking you. And if you tell anyone, she's dead. Then I'll go after Silvia next.

The room spun for a moment.

Oh god, oh god, oh god.

Heart in her throat, she seriously contemplated calling Krystal or even Nick, but this person had broken into her house once without her knowing, had drugged her and dumped her at Henry's. They'd also done something similar outside The End Zone and dumped her at James Reed's. And they knew about the lynx coat and diamond necklace... She hadn't told many people about those.

Now they'd managed to abduct one of her oldest friends.

She had no idea what kind of capabilities they had, but it was clear they were deadly and skilled. So she moved quickly, unlocked her phone and left it on the dresser. Nick would be here soon and hopefully check her phone. She couldn't risk calling him if this person had somehow cloned her phone. But at least she could give him a message.

If they had the capability to track her, she believed they'd done something to her phone.

She forced herself to remain calm—on the outside at least—and grabbed one of the fur coats. Not a lynx, but one of the mink ones. Clover had already taken the lynx coat and the necklace and put them in one of the company's storage units until it was time for the official auction.

Not that any of that mattered now.

She had to be cool and calm if she wanted to sneak out without Arlo realizing. She'd seen him input his pin into his cell the other day and had planned to change his ringtone as a joke.

Now, she needed to steal it before she snuck out of here.

It would be tricky but she'd been nicknamed the "wild Knight" for a reason.

When she got downstairs, she saw that Arlo was talking on his cell phone. He mouthed *Sorry, gonna be a while*, so Berkley simply nodded and went to the refrigerator.

If he was going to be on his phone, she wouldn't be able to steal it. And Kendall couldn't wait. Instead of panicking, she grabbed a bottle of water as if that was the reason she'd come downstairs, then hurried back up with a wave.

Once she was upstairs, she wrote a note to Nick telling him to call Krystal and what was going on. He would be here soon enough for lunch, but she couldn't wait. And she couldn't risk that someone was actually watching her, had cloned her cell phone, knew her every move.

Not to mention if they knew about the lynx coat... Wait, had they been in this house? She glanced around the bedroom, looking for cameras. No, that was ridiculous. Right? But so was the fact that someone had drugged and dumped her at two dead men's houses.

So yeah, maybe not ridiculous. Nothing was out of the realm of possibility at this point. Even leaving a note was taking a risk, but she had no choice. She wrote as quickly as possible, jumped when thunder rumbled outside, shaking the house.

Then she put her unlocked phone onto the dresser, next to the note.

She thought about telling Arlo to call Nick but there were too many ways that could go wrong. She knew he wouldn't let her leave, would physically hold her here until Nick got here.

And that wasn't happening. Not when she had...twenty-seven minutes left.

She slipped on the mink coat, feeling stupid, but it was the easiest way to get it out of here. Once that was done, she slipped a box cutter and her pepper spray into her pockets, palmed her key fob and crept down the stairs.

Her heart was racing the entire time, but when she made it to the main foyer, she paused. She could hear Arlo still talking so he was occupied at least. The two front doors were heavy and creaked so she opened up one of the windows in the sitting room, only to be blasted by a burst of cold air.

Too late to stop now.

She crawled out the window even as she hoped Arlo hadn't heard the gust of wind. Then she eased the window back down most of the way and raced for her car.

He was here to keep her safe, not to stop her from sneaking out. That made this escape a lot easier than it otherwise could have been.

Sprinkles of rain landed on her face as she sprinted across the driveway, but she wasn't stopping. Before jumping into the front seat of her vehicle she shoved the mink coat into the back seat. There was no way she could make the hike to Sanctuary Falls wearing it. Not with the incoming rain.

She didn't even have to put the vehicle Nick insisted she drive right now into neutral to try to back out quietly. Suddenly lightning cracked across the sky, followed by an ominous rumble of thunder, covering the sound of her starting her car.

As she drove down the street, she looked around for anyone watching or tailing her but the rain was too thick now to see much.

Heart in her throat, she gunned it, hoping she didn't spin out in the rain. Because there were only twenty-five minutes left and she wasn't sure she was going to make it in time.

Chapter 30

NICK FROWNED AS HE pulled into the driveway and saw that only Arlo's SUV was there. Ignoring the drenching rain, he threw his truck into park and raced for the closest side door.

Arlo was on the phone as he walked into the kitchen, the other man clearly dealing with something important. Nick pointed upstairs, mouthed Berkley's name.

"Where's her car?" he demanded, not caring that Arlo was on the phone.

Arlo frowned. "Ah, hold on... What?" he asked Nick.

"Berkley's car isn't out front," he snapped before he raced up the stairs. Even as he ran, he called her phone again.

He'd called when he'd reached the street to let her know he was close and she hadn't answered, but he'd assumed she was deep into her work.

When he stepped into the bedroom she'd been working in, everything funneled out around him as he spotted her phone and note on top of a dresser. Cold seeped into his bones as he read the quickly scribbled note.

Phone unlocked. Read my texts from the unknown number. Someone kidnapped Kendall. I think they've hacked my phone. Maybe even have cameras here. I couldn't risk calling anyone or telling Arlo. He would have tried to stop me. I have to get to her in time or they'll kill her. Call my sister, she'll be able to send in backup. Tell them no sirens!

White-hot rage engulfed him as he read the messages, saw the pictures—and now Berkley was on her own against some monster.

Screw that. He saw the location pin, knew exactly where it was.

Arlo cursed behind him. "Nick, I'm sorry—"

"Not now." He'd been aware of Arlo in the room, reading along with him, but he didn't have time for this. Especially if there were cameras in the house.

Though he doubted it. He had security and cameras at the mansion. It was one of the first things he'd done, then after her Bronco had been vandalized he'd added a couple more cameras specifically for the driveway and road. No one had gotten inside.

Which made him wonder who the hell knew about the lynx coat mentioned in the texts.

He sprinted back downstairs. He hadn't told anyone and he knew Berkley was professional enough to keep the coat to herself. Clover knew too, but she wouldn't have told anyone.

Arlo should have seen her leaving on the cameras though and he'd deal with him later.

"Here, pull up the GPS program," Nick said as Arlo slid into the truck with him. "The car she's driving is listed as Black245Fleet."

Arlo was silent as he pulled up the program that listed all vehicles under Nick's construction company. Even though Nick was pissed that he hadn't seen her leave, Arlo was here to keep her safe. He wouldn't have expected her to sneak out.

"She's almost to the Sanctuary Falls trail turnoff," Arlo said quietly.

Nick simply nodded as he called Krystal but she didn't answer so he called Micah next while he scrolled to the ID of the tracking device on the car Berkley was driving. All of his fleet vehicles had GPS installed.

"Hey, everything okay?" Micah asked by way of greeting.

"No." He recapped everything that had happened, then said, "She's got a half-hour head start on us. With this rain she won't be there yet, but she'll be close."

Micah let out a string of curses. "I'm an hour away but I'm heading back now."

"I'm sending you a screenshot of the number that called her. See if you can do anything with it... Krystal's calling." He hung up without waiting for a response.

"Hey, sorry about that, I was in an interview but was just about to call you and Berkley—"

"Berkley's in trouble." Again, he recapped what he knew as he broke multiple traffic laws. By now he was on the two-lane highway that led to the nearest turnoff for the Sanctuary Falls hiking trail. He glanced over as Arlo held up the tablet showing Berkley's car wasn't moving, but it was still turned on. They were close to her now.

"I'm on my way. And we won't use sirens. Keep your phone on you. Are you armed?" Krystal asked.

"Yeah." He kept a pistol in his truck, for the most part because he was at jobsites late into the evening.

"Be careful." She disconnected before he could respond.

"Boss, look. Her car," Arlo said.

He slowed, his windshield wipers doing their best to keep up with the barrage of rain pummeling them. He'd known they were close, couldn't stop the nausea as he prepared for... *No.* Berkley had to be okay.

Turning on his emergency lights, he didn't bother pulling off the side of the road as he threw the truck into park. Her car was halfway in a ditch, the front door and trunk open. And the keys were still in it, he realized, the *ding, ding, ding* alert that the door was open still going off.

He spotted a fur coat in the back seat, and nothing else.

"I think she went this way." Arlo was by the tree line, pointing at impressions of boot prints already filling up with water.

So she hadn't made it to the official parking lot. He wondered if she'd been run off the road or if the rain had forced her into a skid.

Didn't matter, he was going after her.

He just prayed to a god he wasn't sure existed that he wasn't too late.

Chapter 31

SOAKED THROUGH TO HER bones despite wearing a plastic poncho she'd grabbed from the trunk, Berkley couldn't stop shivering as she approached the bottom of Sanctuary Falls. She'd thought about trying to carry the fur coat, but it would have slowed her down even more and it would have gotten ruined in the rain anyway. The kidnapper had demanded it, but she was trying to play the odds. If anything, maybe she could use it as some sort of bargaining chip. She didn't have the diamond necklace so she would just have to lie about that one.

Hiding in the tree line, she scanned the dormant waterfall. It wouldn't be active until March and the pool at the bottom of it was iced over, though it didn't look completely frozen.

She was going to be completely frozen soon though and she wasn't being hyperbolic.

Even though she was well past the deadline, she hoped the lunatic who'd kidnapped Kendall would...ugh, what? Show some grace? *Damn it.*

This was all a mess. She'd been racing to get here and had lost control, swerved into a ditch with no way to get out.

But she had to save her friend—she just hoped Nick had seen her note by now and that he and Krystal were on the way.

She patted one pocket, felt the box cutter in it. Her other pocket bulged with her pepper spray. It wasn't going anywhere. Though she wasn't sure it even worked anyway. Not with how soaked she was.

Squinting against the pounding rain, she scanned the front of the falls, couldn't see anyone or anything that stood out.

The only way to get to the interior of the falls was from the back. A hike she'd made countless times. Again, just not in the winter or in the pouring rain.

Though she wanted to head straight there, she decided to go around, using the woods as cover. Someone was waiting for her and she couldn't just face them head on.

They'd clearly planned for this, likely had a gun.

The Sanctuary Falls Sheriff's Department was a decent size and their people had a lot of former military. She knew they were trained.

But she had no idea when backup would get here so she couldn't depend on anyone but herself now.

Her boots made sucking sounds as she tried to hurry. She trudged through the thick muck, hiking upward to the west where the best entrance to the top of the falls was.

From her position, she could see the back of the falls now. There was an overhanging boulder over it that created an open cave area. It was partially open above, but the curve of it protected anyone inside from the rain. In the picture of Kendall, she'd recognized some of the older graffiti in the background.

There was also a huge opening that connected to the front of the waterfall, but that was just a steep drop-off with no way to climb up it.

She just hoped whoever had taken her friend was expecting her to come to the front of the falls where they'd pinned the location, and not around the back entrance. The rain was slowing her down, but it might be the only thing that gave her the element of surprise.

Breathing hard, she crouched down between two pine trees planted way too close together. The rain was still coming down hard, but had let up enough for her to see...

Someone in a navy hooded jacket and thick waterproof pants stepped out of the hidden boulder area.

They glanced around, but didn't pause when they scanned past where Berkley was hiding. Probably because she was slightly elevated and the rain was doing a damn good job of providing cover.

The hooded person looked around again, then stalked toward the main trail. She couldn't tell if it was a man or woman, given the bulky coat, but the person was tall. So she was leaning toward this being a man.

Her heart jumped in her throat. This might be her only chance to save Kendall.

Once the hooded person moved out of sight, she went for it. Instead of trying to hike down, she sat on her butt and slid down the muddy incline. She bit back a cry when she rolled over a jagged root and kept going until she could stand.

Heart pounding, she pulled out her box cutter and hurried toward the cave opening. The minute she stepped inside it was like entering an insulated box.

The noise from the rain was muffled, which only made the squishes from her muddy boots all the louder to her ears.

As she rounded the corner and stepped deeper into the cave, she paused at the distinctive scent of Black Opium.

Inhaled again.

Then she spotted her friend tied up in the corner and sucked in a breath. *What the hell?*

Chapter 32

NICK AND ARLO FROZE behind a tree when they spotted two clearly armed men trekking down the hiking trail.

The armed men were both in camo pants, matching waterproof hooded jackets, and heavy-duty boots. Clearly prepared for the weather and environment.

And they were carrying assault rifles with ease.

Rain and excess water was bad for weapons in general and increased the chance of malfunction, but none of that mattered now. He and Arlo had to get close enough to these guys to incapacitate them. Kill them if necessary.

Because these men weren't hunters. Gun season had ended a couple weeks ago and this was connected to a national park.

No, whoever had lured Berkley here was working with these guys, he'd bet everything he owned on it.

He looked at Arlo, who was hunkered down behind a tree ten feet away.

Arlo nodded when Nick motioned with his hands. They'd never served together, but they were both former military and had enough experience to take down two assholes.

Using the rain to cover their sound, they made it to the next layer of trees.

The men stopped ahead of them, one of them talking into a radio.

Nick was too far away to hear what the person on the other end said, but could hear the man's response.

"No one's come through here yet. Yeah, I'm sure." The man looked up and down the trail, as if the person on the other end could see them. "I'm telling you, no one has come through. And there's been no sign of the cops at the parking area."

He had a lot of questions, but the answers didn't matter much since he knew that whoever had lured Berkley here wasn't working alone.

She hadn't made it to the parking lot, and maybe that had saved her since she'd gone into the woods on foot from a different direction. No one seemed to know she was here.

And he had no doubt she was. They'd followed her boot prints as far as they could before the rain had fully washed them away. She'd been heading for the main falls.

Nick and Arlo kept moving closer while the two men were stationary and distracted by the radio call.

Only five feet away now, with two oak trees giving them cover.

The guy shoved his radio back into its holder then pulled his jacket back over it. He muttered something to his buddy but it was too low to hear.

The other guy laughed.

Neither of them had their weapons up at the ready and their backs were to him and Arlo.

Nick looked once at Arlo, nodded.

They moved in unison, Arlo attacking the guy on the left, Nick the one on the right.

It was impossible to be completely silent this close. The men turned at the last second, but it was too late.

Nick attacked his target before he'd fully turned, had his forearm around the man's neck, his other forearm locking his head in place as he choked him out.

The man dropped his weapon and tried to attack Nick with his hands.

He should have gone for a knife, tried to stab Nick's thigh, but he was losing oxygen too fast, his legs thrashing around, his hands making wild gestures before he slumped into a dead weight.

Arlo had disarmed and knocked out the other man as well, had him face-down on the muddy path. "We need to move them off the trail," he said even as Nick had the same idea.

He hauled his guy deeper into the woods, then took the man's radio and the rest of his weapons. The assault rifles were too bulky for their needs so they hid them while the men were still passed out.

"Stay with them until they wake up, see if you can get anything out of them." Like who the hell they were working with.

Arlo started binding their wrists with belts as Nick trained his SIG on the two men. They were propped up against the trunk of a two-hundred-year-old oak and wouldn't be going anywhere.

"I got them. Go, find her."

He didn't need to tell Nick twice. Carrying the radio, he turned the volume on low and tucked it under his own jacket.

At least now he knew there were potentially more men out here as lookouts. So he quickly texted Krystal to tell her about the lookout at the parking lot. He didn't want anyone alerted that Berkley had backup.

Whoever had taken her was going to pay.

Chapter 33

Berkley wasn't sure what she was seeing. Or more accurately, why Silvia was in the cave, tied up and gagged. When she'd smelled Silvia's Black Opium she'd thought... Well, she hadn't thought she'd be walking into this.

Her friend's eyes were wide with fear as she approached, box cutter in hand.

Silvia shook her head wildly, trying to talk behind her mouth covering.

Berkley wasn't sure if she heard the noise or her instinct kicked in, but she ducked and rolled as the sound of a bat whistled by her head.

On her back for only a second, she scrambled away, staring in horror as Kendall stood there holding a bat, her eyes wild with rage. She also wasn't wounded, no swollen eye, nothing like in the pictures she'd seen.

She also realized she'd dropped her box cutter. But she still had her pepper spray.

When she went to grab it from her pocket, Kendall whipped out a pistol and dropped her bat with a loud clatter, the sound echoing in the wide cave.

"Drop it on the ground, kick it away," Kendall ordered. Her eyes might be crazy, but her voice was deadly calm.

And so was the grip on her weapon.

Trembling from the cold and a whole lot of fear, Berkley managed to pull it out of her front pocket and tossed it away. It bounced off one of the walls with a rattle but she didn't dare take her eyes off Kendall.

"I'm impressed you managed to avoid my men," her friend—former!—said.

Men?

"But I know not to take anything you do for granted. Especially after you didn't call the cops at Reed's house." She sounded mildly impressed.

Berkley blinked. "Wait... *You* killed Reed? And Henry?" What alternate universe was she in right now? Out of the corner of her eye she could see that Silvia had quietly grabbed the box cutter and was working on freeing her bindings. Berkley needed to keep all the attention on her until Silvia was free.

"Of course I did. Jesus, you should be thanking me," Kendall snarled. Her white-blonde hair was pulled back in a tight braid, and even with the waterproof hoodie jacket, her hair and face were damp.

"Thank you for trying to set me up for murder?"

Kendall's mouth curved up in a semblance of a smile, but all Berkley saw was a shark. As if a mask had fallen away. Which clearly it had, because she didn't recognize this woman staring back at her as if she was prey. As if Berkley disgusted her.

"Why did you kill them?" she whispered, angry at herself for not being able to shout the question. But it was as if her entire world had shifted, the foundation crumbling underneath her feet.

She'd been friends with Kendall since she was thirteen. Silvia since she was six. *Oh god, Silvia, keep cutting those bindings!*

"Because I wanted to." Spit flew from her mouth as she snarled the words. "Men are all the same. Every single one of them deserve what they get."

"So you're like...a serial killer?" Were those words actually coming out of her mouth right now?

Kendall sniffed once. "Technically, sure. But this isn't about that."

What the hell was *this* or *that*? "Oookay." She could see that Silvia was almost free.

Unfortunately the pistol hadn't wavered in Kendall's grip once. At least all her focus was on Berkley. Maybe Silvia would still have a chance.

Kendall rolled her eyes when Berkley didn't say more. "I've taken out way more than your obnoxious ex-husband and that sniveling monkey Reed."

"Why?"

"Because they all underestimated me, that's why! Henry thought he could screw me and discard me just like he did with *you*." Disdain dripped from every word as she looked Berkley up and down.

So they'd hooked up. Not important, but it still cut deep to know her friend— *Nope*. Kendall was *not* her friend. She was a monster in human clothing, that much was clear. Maybe she'd never known her at all.

"Is that why you killed Reed too? And why did you dump me at his house? I don't even know him."

She held up a finger with her free hand, then pulled out a radio from under her jacket. "Everything still clear?" she asked.

"All clear," a male voice responded.

Looking satisfied, she tucked it away again. "I killed Reed because he was skimming off the top of *my* profits. I did that asshole a favor by letting him run pills for me. He needed to pay off a debt to another asshole and couldn't afford it. So, problem solver that I am, I offered him an easy solution. Instead of being *grateful*, he got greedy. Typical man," she muttered, shaking her head.

So Kendall was selling drugs on top of killing people for fun? "And Henry?"

She lifted a shoulder. "He found out about my operation and wanted a cut. Threatened to turn me in if I didn't give him fifty percent. *Fifty. Percent.*" Pure outrage filled her voice.

"The audacity," Berkley said dryly, voice shaking. Also, what freaking operation? She had so many questions but wasn't sure how long she could keep Kendall distracted and talking.

"Right?" It was like Kendall didn't even hear the sarcasm.

"Why did you set me up? I thought we were friends." God, why did her voice have to sound so small?

Kendall rolled her eyes. "We were never friends. You *used* to be fun," she added. "But we weren't friends. Then you had to marry that asshole. God, he was even a lousy lay." She shook herself again, shuddered. "And I set you up because I was so tired of your self-righteousness. You healed after Henry, oh my god, we all get it! You think you're so much better than me and I'm over it. So when you messed up my plan with Reed, I decided it would make more sense to dump you at Henry's. I figured for sure the cops would take you down for that one and I'd kill two birds with one stone."

"You want me in jail?" Otherwise Kendall could have just killed her at any time. She'd let the woman in her house... Kendall had known her security code, had free access to her house at any time. Oh god, she was going to be sick.

"I'm so tired of your holier-than-thou bullshit. You turned your life around and act insufferable about it."

Even though it wasn't true, the words still hit their mark. She tried to keep her expression neutral, but knew her hurt must have shown because Kendall smirked.

"Why bring Silvia into it though?" she asked when Kendall made a move to turn around.

Kendall made a little tsking sound. "Because someone couldn't mind their own business—"

"Shut up!" Silvia screamed as she lunged, blade raised.

Kendall spun fast, so Berkley threw herself at her former friend.

The gun went off, a cracking boom echoing in the cave as she tackled Kendall to the hard ground.

Kendall screamed and swung out at Berkley, still clutching her gun.

Silvia wasn't moving, but Berkley couldn't focus on her. Couldn't even risk looking in her direction as she grabbed Kendall's arm and slammed it to the ground with a scream of rage and terror.

She didn't let go, so Berkley bit down on her forearm as rage punched through her.

Kendall screamed and dropped the gun.

Before Berkley could get her bearings, pain exploded in her skull when Kendall punched her.

Berkley loosened her grip and Kendall scrambled away. Dove for the gun.

Berkley moved faster, kicking out at it since she couldn't grab it.

The gun skittered into the entryway to the waterfall cliff.

When Kendall jumped up and stumbled after it, Berkley forced herself to her feet even as her temple throbbed. She thought she heard movement behind her, hoped Silvia was okay. But there was no time to check.

As Kendall bent down to grab the gun, the opening of the dry waterfall behind her, Berkley launched herself at the woman she'd never really known.

Kendall screamed as she was knocked off-balance, tumbled over the edge.

Berkley wasn't sure what compelled her to reach out but she did, trying to stop Kendall from falling to her death. Stupid instinct kicking in.

She needed to pay for her crimes, to face justice.

Dangling over the edge, Kendall held tight to Berkley's forearm, digging her fingers in tight as she thrashed with her whole body.

She was going to pull them both down if she didn't stop.

"Stop moving!" Berkley shouted. "You'll fall." The only reason she had the strength to hold her up was because of all the bouldering she'd been doing the last year.

"I'm not going to jail," Kendall screamed at her, thrashing wilder as she tightened her grip even more. Her nails sliced into Berkley's arms, digging deep.

Oh god. She was going to take Berkley down with her. She clawed at the woman's fingers, trying to tear free, but Kendall's grip was like steel as Berkley slipped farther and farther forward.

Kendall was a dead weight now, dragging them both to their deaths—

Nick was suddenly there, lying flat next to Berkley, the discarded box cutter in hand.

"No!" Kendall screamed.

But it was too late. He stabbed straight into Kendall's hand, forcing her to let go with another short-lived scream.

Berkley stared in horror as the woman she'd once known, once loved, fell onto the frozen ice below with a sickening crack of bones and… Her body began to sink below the ice as the shattered pieces shifted and moved under the brutal impact.

"Don't look." Nick hauled her backward, practically dragged her away from the deadly drop.

Exhausted, she crawled back a few feet then forced herself to her feet on shaky legs even as it hit her that he was here. He'd come for her. "Silvia!" she suddenly shouted.

"She's alive." He held on to her hand, tugged her back into the open cave to find Silvia struggling to her feet as she clutched the side of her head.

"Are you okay?" Standing in front of her friend, Berkley tried to see how deep the wound was.

"I'm pissed, but fine," Silvia said, then paused. "Actually I'm not fine. But we're alive and she can't hurt anyone anymore."

As the tears started to fall, Nick's arms wrapped around both her and Silvia.

"You guys are going to be okay," he murmured and that was when she realized Silvia was crying too.

Of course she was.

And she didn't care that he was holding her too tight as she squeezed both him and Silvia. The nightmare was over. They were alive. And Kendall's broken body was lying under the ice.

Chapter 34

"I HAVE SO MANY questions," Berkley murmured from where she leaned against the back of the ambulance.

She was a combination of exhaustion and kind of like she wanted to puke all at once. Maybe—probably—she was in shock.

Now in the small parking lot at the start of the Sanctuary Falls hiking trail, there were four cop cars, two ambulances, and a bunch of FBI agents all moving at once. It was chaos for her eyes and brain.

Four different men had been handcuffed and placed in the back of shiny black SUVs and taken away. Apparently they'd worked with—or for, she still wasn't sure—Kendall.

"We're going to get answers." Krystal looked more worried than Berkley had ever seen her. She'd barely blinked since she'd arrived and hadn't moved more than two feet away from her. "And you really need to go to the hospital. The Feds are going to want to talk to you, but I think you should get officially checked out first."

The EMT who was loading up some supplies cleared her throat. Loudly. "That's what I said."

Because Berkley had refused to get on one of the stretchers. But she was wrapped up in one of the mylar blankets in a change of clean—and more importantly, *dry*—clothes. And the rain had finally stopped, so talk about a small miracle. She was probably going to go to the hospital but only because it was clear Silvia was going to have to and she wasn't letting her friend go alone.

One of the EMTs was putting a bandage on Silvia's forehead while she sat against the back of the other ambulance, looking more pissed than hurt.

The Feds on scene had instructed them to separate and had taken Nick away to question him. She guessed it was so they couldn't "get their stories straight" or whatever, but they'd been alone for about fifteen minutes before the cavalry had arrived so that ship had sailed.

Not that it mattered. They didn't have anything to get straight.

They were all just going to tell the truth.

Kendall had kidnapped Silvia, lured Berkley here, and Nick had followed.

She understood that the FBI had to question all of them, but she hated that she couldn't be with Nick right now. He kept throwing her looks from where he stood twenty feet away with two FBI agents and she could see the annoyance on that handsome face. Yeah, he was about done with them.

And she just wanted to bury her face against his chest. He'd come for her, had saved her life. If he hadn't arrived when he had, that lunatic would have taken her over the edge and she wouldn't be standing here right now.

"Hey, why is Apollo here?" She nudged Krystal, who'd been texting on her phone. She knew that Nick had told Micah—who'd disappeared five minutes ago—but he hadn't called Apollo.

Her sister looked up and they both watched as he talked to one of the officers standing by the crime scene tape.

To her surprise, the guy lifted the tape and Apollo stalked across the parking lot toward them like a man on a mission. "Did you call him? I mean, it's kind of sweet that he's here..." Instead of heading their way, Apollo veered off and...oh. "Um, oh my god, are you seeing what I'm seeing?"

"If you're asking if Apollo is currently kissing Silvia like they're the last two people on earth, then yes, I'm seeing it too." Krystal looked just as surprised as Berkley felt.

As she stared, Micah appeared out of nowhere, carrying a steaming to-go cup of something. "Figured hot chocolate would warm you up even faster. And they've been trying to hide things for months. Apparently they're out in the open now. I called him because I knew he'd want to be here," he added.

"You knew about this?" Berkley and Krystal asked at the same time as the three of them stood and stared like weirdos at her best friend and her older brother just full-on making out.

"Yeah. I helped him pick out her Christmas gift."

"I will kill you later for not sharing," Berkley murmured as she took a sip. "Or maybe just hurt you a little because this is good." And she was pretty sure she was still in shock.

It was impossible to wrap her mind around the fact that her friend was a killer and drug dealer who had tried to set her up for murder. According to Silvia, Kendall had planned to kill Silvia, make it look like Berkley had done it, then make Berkley's death look like a suicide from jumping off the waterfall. And she'd had men watching out for Berkley's arrival—men from her drug running operation. Something else that Berkley was having a hard time wrapping her mind around.

She didn't think she would ever understand Kendall's motivation, or what had been wrong with her. Or how she'd missed the signs for all these years.

But as Nick stepped up to her, wrapped his arms around her shoulders and pulled her against him, she realized she didn't have to understand or know everything at that moment.

Because she was in his arms and that was the only place she wanted to be.

Chapter 35

THREE DAYS LATER

"Stop staring," Silvia muttered, her cheeks turning pink.

Berkley just grinned at her friend from across Nick's dining room table. "I'm not staring. It's just going to take some getting used to, seeing you guys together." She looked between Silvia and Apollo. "Though if you end up—"

"Don't say it." Silvia brandished her fork in Berkley's direction as Nick stepped back into the room carrying a bottle of red wine. "Do not even think it."

Grinning, Nick topped off Berkley's glass then did the same for Silvia's when she held hers up and waved it around impatiently.

"How did you know what I was going to say?" Berkley asked as Nick sat next to her. She'd been about to say if they ended up married, they'd be sisters for real.

"Everyone knows what you were going to say, dumbass," Apollo murmured in typical big brother form, sliding an arm around Silvia's shoulders possessively. Berkley had never seen him like this. "And who knows what the future will bring." He started humming the "Wedding March," and the look he gave Silvia...

Nope, not touching that, Berkley thought. It was too weird. Good weird, but the last few days had been a lot to process.

A *whoooole* lot.

"Don't call your sister a dumbass," Silvia murmured, but there was no heat in her voice and her cheeks had flushed crimson as he continued humming that obnoxious tune.

Well, then. They were *serious* serious.

She wondered where she and Nick were on that same serious scale, but hadn't wanted to ask. Mostly because she hadn't wanted the wrong answer. But also because she'd been enjoying just sleeping and having sex the last few days.

Clover stepped back into the room carrying a strawberry-covered chocolate cake. "Figured everyone could use dessert. Picked this up from Brunch and Bliss this morning, so you know it's good."

They'd already eaten dinner—takeout, because no one was doing any cooking the last few days. And dessert sounded perfect.

"You're a goddess," Berkley murmured, wishing she could just dig her fork right into the cake and eat the whole thing herself.

Clover grinned. "There's strawberry buttercream filling on the inner layers."

Yep, definitely a goddess.

When the doorbell rang, Clover headed to get it before any of them could move, even though it was Nick's place. Probably because Krystal had called half an hour ago and told them she was headed over.

With news.

Three days later after...*everything*, and Berkley still found herself trying to wrap her mind around the fact that Kendall had hated her enough to try to set her up for murder. To actually kill people and run drugs throughout the state and beyond.

Her operation had been relatively small, but it had been growing. And if it hadn't been for her murder spree catching the eye of the FBI, they seemed to think she'd have grown exponentially in the next two years. It was going to take a while for the Feds to uncover her entire operation and who she'd been working with at the hospital, but she'd used her knowledge of the inner workings to her advantage.

Like a total psychopath.

Krystal had been trickling information to Berkley the last few days and she was grateful to get it in little bits. Made it easier to digest.

Mostly, anyway.

Moments later Krystal walked in with Micah, which was surprising but not unwelcome, and two FBI agents.

They were in casual clothes, but she'd already answered what felt like a thousand questions from Special Agents Raine and Bush. In looks, they were complete opposite. Raine was a tall, beautiful woman and Bush an older man who couldn't be more than five feet two. They'd been nothing but kind to her and she was grateful they'd used kid gloves during her questioning.

Later she'd realized that of course she'd been in shock after watching Kendall plummet to her death. So of course they were kind to her. But she appreciated it all the same.

She and Nick both started to stand, but Raine just shook her head. "Sit, please."

"Do you want some coffee and cake?" Nick asked.

Raine politely shook her head. "No, but thank you."

"I mean, we could take it to go," Bush murmured.

The look Raine gave him was familiar and amused, making it clear they'd worked together a long time.

"Done," Nick said. "And please sit."

Krystal sat next to Berkley and the two agents ended up standing at the end of the table. Micah disappeared into the kitchen with Clover, and Berkley was going to ask him later what the heck was going on with the two of them because she wasn't so sure it was romantic. Right now, however, she could only handle so much information.

"We're heading out of town tomorrow and just wanted to check in and thank you again for answering all our questions," Bush said.

"We also wanted to update you a little and hopefully give you some closure." Raine cleared her throat. "Some of this will come out in the news later and I wouldn't be surprised if someone made a documentary about Kendall Bond." She shook her head in annoyance. "As of right now we have her tied to twelve murders. We're already working to get at least two convictions we think she was actually responsible for overturned and we're not getting any pushback. I think once we dig back even further, there will be more."

Berkley stared at her in shock. *More than twelve...*

"A couple pets in her neighborhood were murdered when we were high school seniors," Silvia murmured.

"What?" Berkley glanced at her friend in surprise.

Silvia nodded. "I thought about it earlier when we were walking Sunshine."

Hearing her name, Sunshine trotted over to the table and set her head on Silvia's lap.

"That's right," Krystal murmured. "I remember hearing about that. They were killed with antifreeze or something."

Berkley's stomach tightened as she wondered if Kendall had been behind that too. Because she'd thought about the fact that Sunshine had left the guest bedroom when Kendall had arrived the other night. She'd just assumed Sunshine had wanted to be with her owner, but maybe there had been more to it. Dogs had a sense of people.

Raine's expression was grim. "That tracks with our profile of her. If either of you think of anything else, please let us know. Female serial killers are rare so we want to be accurate with her profile. But you're both safe. Her entire operation has been shut down—or it's being shut down—and the men and women who worked for her had nothing to do with you."

"She said that Henry found out about her operation," Berkley said, still not sure if Kendall had been lying. The woman had lied about so much.

Clearly.

"From what we can tell, he had found out. They had a short-lived relation-ship after your divorce and apparently there was bad blood between them. We confirmed that from multiple people at the hospital. We've also discov-ered that she was spreading rumors about you at the hospital." Raine looked at Berkley. "Now that she's been outed as a serial killer and drug runner, I'm sure people will take anything she said with a grain of salt."

So instead of standing up for her, of course Kendall had been fueling ru-mors. Nausea swelled inside Berkley for a moment. "And she really knocked people out and just dumped them at her murder victims' houses?"

"Yep," Raine said. "And she's not the only killer who's done this. She took DNA from hospital trash and sprinkled it at all her crime scenes as a way to screw with investigators. Or that's our working theory. It was like a calling card, we think. That's neither here nor there though. You and Silvia aren't in any danger now. No one else is coming after you."

Krystal squeezed her hand for support and Nick squeezed her shoulder. Berkley was grateful her family and Nick were here to support both her and Silvia.

"Was she involved with Louis Cain?" Berkley knew that her sister had questioned him and Kendall had said something about Reed owing someone money.

"No. Not directly anyway. But they had crossover customers and she hired away some of his people." Raine looked at Krystal, then at Berkley, and she wasn't sure she could read the agent's expression as she said, "Cain hasn't been arrested for anything. He was very helpful in handing over any and all information on Ms. Bond."

Ah, so he'd cut some sort of deal and likely had immunity. Or maybe he was now a confidential informant or snitch or whatever it was called. Whatever, the man wasn't a threat to them and she could only hope that the cops would bring him down eventually. That was a problem for the future.

The special agents left not long after, then Krystal and Micah left. The other three trickled out after demolishing the rest of the cake, and then it was just Berkley, Nick and Sunshine.

In his kitchen, Berkley stepped into Nick's arms, buried her face against his chest as he wrapped his arms around her. "I feel like I can finally breathe again," she murmured, turning her face to the side, listening to the steady beat of his heart.

"What do you say about taking the rest of the week off and not leaving my house?"

She laughed lightly. "I think I might go stir-crazy...but I'll take tomorrow off and start back Wednesday."

"Fine, but I'll be working with you."

She leaned back to look up at him. "Seriously? I promise not to sneak off again," she said, aiming for teasing, but it fell flat.

"I know, but I'm not ready to let you out of my sight."

"I guess I can't complain about that," she murmured, her gaze falling to his mouth.

"Before we get naked, can we just...talk?" he asked, maybe reading the intention in her eyes.

"Talk?"

He snickered. "You don't have to sound so deflated by that."

She lifted a shoulder. "I'm just kidding. And I want to do whatever you want. I'm just happy to...be alive. I still can't believe that I never knew her at all. At this point I'm questioning my instinct. I didn't see what a monster she was. Or Henry."

"Don't do that," he said as he led her to the living room where his fireplace was going strong.

Sunshine threw herself onto one of the many dog beds strewn around the house and stretched out in front of it while the two of them cuddled up on his couch.

"It's hard not to question myself."

"You already know this, but he was actively hiding who he was from you. Clearly so was Kendall. And not just from you, but from Silvia and most people who knew her. She sounds like an actual psychopath. Or sociopath. I don't know the difference."

"There were...I don't even know if I'd call them red flags, but she could be mean sometimes. Just say thoughtless stuff and follow up with 'I'm joking.' Or more often than not she'd let Silvia or me pay for stuff when we were all out. It annoyed Silvia more than me." She paused. "Okay it annoyed me too, but Kendall and I were both sort of screw-ups when we were younger, so I felt, I guess, I don't know, an affinity to her. We both turned our lives around and... Well that's a lie. She was nothing I thought she was."

He kissed the top of her head as she curled into him. "I didn't understand this until recently but my dad must have worn quite the mask to get my mom to marry him." His voice was low, his tone pensive. "I hate to admit this, but I blamed her for staying. And now I can see that she was a victim. We all were. We were all just trying to cope. And he hid that side of himself from the rest of the world. Everyone else thought he was this perfect family man. They had no idea who the real monster was. I guess I'm telling you because...monsters are *really good* at hiding who they are."

She was quiet for a long moment, glad he'd opened up to her, then whispered, "I feel guilty for being glad she's gone. That I won't have to go through a trial. That I won't have to look at her lying face again."

"Pretty sure that's normal." He kissed her head again and she just wanted to soak up all of his kisses and affection.

"Is it okay if we don't talk about her for a while? Or at least the rest of the night?" She looked up at him now.

He must have read her expression clearly, because he grinned. "So no more talking at all?"

"You can talk...as long as you get naked while doing it."

He let out a bark of laughter. "I like that I never know what's going to come out of your mouth. I will say one more thing... I'm falling for you, Berkley. The way I feel about you... Pretty sure it's already love."

She stared in shock at his declaration.

"You don't have to say anything," he continued, brushing his lips over hers. "I just wanted to put it out there."

Warmth spread throughout her, all the way to her toes, at his words. "For the record, I'm falling for you too." She was pretty sure she was already there, even if it was way too soon. But she'd been through a lot and was going to grab onto life.

Because it could all end tomorrow and she didn't want to have any regrets. So she kissed the man she'd definitely fallen for and forgot about the outside world for a while.

Chapter 36

Clover frowned as Micah barreled his way into her house. She'd left her brother's place hours ago and had hoped she'd managed to avoid the conversation Micah was determined to have with her. "Yes, please come in," she gritted out. She was about done with the men in her life just taking over.

"Our conversation from before isn't finished." He turned to face her, looking all adorable, and ugh, she hated that she'd kissed him once.

Biggest mistake of her life. Because now she knew what his lips felt like against hers, how damn good he kissed. And she wondered if that translated to other things. The man was so damn smart he'd probably read all there was to know on pleasuring a woman before he'd even had sex the first time— Oh my god she had to stop! *Stop, stop, stop,* she ordered.

"Are you even listening to me?" he demanded, his green eyes laser focused on her.

She turned away from him and stalked to her living room, mostly because she needed to get her dumb brain under control.

He followed her and when she turned she found him staring. He blinked once. Twice. "What the hell is this?"

"It's called laundry." And fine, she was playing catch-up for weeks so her couches were quite literally covered in her clothes and towels. She'd also washed her bed linens and curtains because that was what she did when stressed, so there was even more than normal. "How about you help instead of just staring?" she snipped, not expecting him to actually pitch in.

But he dove right into a pile of towels and started folding—the correct way. Not the lazy way. *Huh.*

"Why are you staring at me?"

"I'm just impressed you know how to fold towels."

"I feel like I should probably be insulted, but other than my brothers, most of my friends let their laundry pile up like...you." His tone was dry.

"Hey!"

"I'm just playing." His lip quirked up ever so slightly, and damn it, she wanted to kiss him again.

"So why are you here?" She knew, but she wanted him to start talking. Because the faster he did, the faster he could leave.

"Because you made it sound like you were going to go after Louis Cain by yourself and that would be a big mistake."

"I'm not going to go after him." She was just stalking him a little bit. Or a lot. Because she was convinced he'd had something to do with her friend's disappearance. Or maybe even...murder.

Something Clover was trying hard not to think about, even though it made sense. A horrible, horrible, sense.

"I can hear the lie in your voice." He moved fast, already done with the stack of towels, and had moved on.

"Don't touch my...stuff!"

He held up a hot pink thong, eyebrows raised, then set it back on the couch, but yeah, she saw the heat in his gaze.

"It's never happening!" she shouted, then winced. Seriously, what the hell was wrong with her? Oh, so much, she knew that.

Micah paused, watching her with those intense green eyes she wanted to lose herself in. "Me touching your panties?"

"No. I mean, yes. But nothing is happening between us. I know I kissed you, but that was a mistake. And it won't be happening again."

"You didn't like it?"

She blinked, but then forced her expression to go full-on haughty. "Not really." She felt bad lying, but not *that* bad. Not when he was just so damn distracting.

His eyes narrowed so she ignored him and picked up a pair of jogging pants.

"Anyway," she continued, hoping he'd drop it, "you don't have to worry about me chasing down Cain, so you can just...not worry about me."

He grunted and fluffed out one of her curtains, glanced around the living room. "Was this set over there?"

She nodded and he disappeared into her garage, came back in with a ladder and hung up her curtains for her while she continued folding. "Are you going to say anything else?"

"I'm trying to choose my words carefully. I know you're lying to me about not going after Cain. Because I know you've been following him. And before you ask how I know, I've been following you."

Her mouth fell open before she could stop herself. "What!"

He shrugged, completely unapologetic as he climbed down the ladder. "Not going to apologize, if that's what you're waiting for. Because let me remind you that *you* came to me asking for help."

"I know I did...but you can just forget everything."

"That's not going to happen. And since it's clear that you're going to run straight into danger, you're going to work with me."

She started to argue but then paused. "Explain."

"I never stopped digging into him. Unfortunately it sounds like he's got federal protection. Or at the very least he's a CI for the FBI. Which won't give him immunity, but...if he's feeding the Feds enough information to take down bigger fish, they'll keep him protected to an extent."

She inwardly cursed.

"So we'll just have to be smarter than him and the Feds if you want to bring him down."

"I just want to find my friend," she whispered.

"I know." The expression on his face said that he really did understand and care.

And that hit her right in the chest. "So you're not going to cut me out? You're going to let me help you bring him down?"

He sighed and picked up one of her kitchen towels, began folding. "I'll help you find your friend. But you've got to listen to me. You can't just run off and do your own thing. Cain is too dangerous for that. And so are the people he works with."

"Then don't keep me in the dark 'for my own good,'" she said in a slightly mocking tone. "And I won't have a reason to do things on my own."

"Fine." His jaw clenched and it looked as if he wanted to say more but then he simply picked up another hand towel and began folding.

Okay, then. That was that. They were going to figure out what happened to her friend Ilena. And if it turned out Cain had been involved in her disappearance...they'd cross that bridge when they got to it.

Epilogue

TWO MONTHS LATER

BERKLEY WALKED through the uncluttered sitting room with Nick by her side. "I can't believe I'm finally done." Was that a hint of wistfulness in her voice? Why yes it was. She was really going to miss working inside the Carmine Mansion.

She'd found a jewel-toned rug rolled and wrapped up in the attic in basically new condition, so she'd moved the dark teal and purple rug into the sitting room. Instead of going heavy on the dark-colored walls, she'd ended up having them painted a lighter color and used a lot of jewel tones in the decorations. She thought of it as more modern Victorian, because while she loved color, she wanted the space to feel bigger. And this way the future owner would be able to imagine their own belongings in place.

"You did an incredible job." Nick slid his hand into hers as they approached the bay of windows overlooking the front yard and quiet street. "You're amazing."

"Well I can't hear that enough," she murmured.

It might be officially spring, but the weather hadn't shifted yet and there was still a chill in the air. When spring finally hit, however, the yard was going to be as stunning as the interior—full of color and life.

It had taken her a little over a month to catalogue everything, then Nick and Clover had needed to decide what they wanted to keep for the sale. Though they'd asked her opinion for everything, and if she said it needed to stay, it stayed. She wasn't sure if it was because she was dating Nick—and staying at his place basically every night—or if they trusted her opinion so much, but she'd had a heavy hand in getting the mansion ready for sale. Much more than she normally did with other auctions.

Either way, the house was stunning. And she would live in it if possible. You know, if she could actually afford it. "So when are you going to put it on the market?"

"We already have an offer." His deep voice pulled her attention to him.

Not that it was ever fully off the gorgeous man. If he was anywhere nearby, he owned part of her attention.

"Wait, what?" She blinked up at him. "Already? I mean, I guess I'm not surprised, but that was fast." She tried to keep that stupid disappointed note out of her voice. This was a good thing! She'd already been contacted by four different companies who restored historic homes, asking for her help.

Word of mouth was spreading about this project—and the fact that she'd been linked to a murderous monster in the national news probably wasn't hurting the spreading of her name. She'd officially hired Dana full-time to keep up with all the admin stuff and to filter out the jerks who only wanted to meet her because of what had happened.

"I realize this is fast," Nick said as he slid down on one knee.

"Well yeah, but that's a good thing... Wait, why are you..." She stared as he pulled out a small box with the symbol of a local jeweler on the front and opened it to reveal a vintage art deco sapphire engagement ring. A gasp escaped as she realized what was happening and she stared at him.

For the first time since she'd met him, he actually looked nervous. "Like I said, I know it's fast, but we can have a long engagement. I love you, Berkley, and I hope you'll marry me."

"I love you too. And yes." She didn't even have to think about it. After her first experience, she'd never thought she'd want to get married again, but that had taught her everything she *didn't* want.

And everything she did want. Which was Nick Storm.

His smile was infectious as he slid the ring on her finger. "Now that you've said yes... This is our house. You already know Sunshine loves it too."

That sweet dog absolutely loved it, had picked out her favorite spot in the sitting room every time she came over. "What!" She couldn't stop the shout that escaped. "Are you serious!" Still shouting. *Come on girl, get yourself under control.*

Grinning, he stood and pulled her into his arms. "This is your place. You belong here—we belong here. I didn't lead with the house because I wanted to make sure you wanted to marry me for me," he said on a laugh.

"I think you're only partially joking." She slid her arms around him, her heart so full she could barely stand it. This was their place? Oh god, he'd been smart to lead with the proposal.

"Oh, I'm not." Leaning down, he brushed his lips over hers. "Since you said yes, we can expect your family over in an hour for a celebration."

"You told my family first?"

"I didn't mean to. I just asked Krystal for her opinion on the ring, and she told Apollo, who told—"

"Silvia and likely Micah, who told Cormac."

He snickered. "That's exactly right. In that order. Apparently I have a lot to learn about your family."

"You really do. I seriously love you so much. With or without this house, I love you."

"Well in that case—"

"Don't say it. Don't even joke it." They were keeping this place.

He grinned down at her, his gunmetal gray eyes full of mischief. "I would never."

"Think we have enough time before everyone gets here?" She didn't specify what she meant because he knew exactly what her intentions were by now.

His eyes heated at her question. Then he kissed her and she had her answer as they lost themselves in each other.

—THE END—

Dear Readers

THANK YOU SO MUCH for reading Knight's Storm, the first book in the all new Sanctuary Falls series! If you'd like to stay in touch and be the first to learn about new releases, feel free to check out my website:

https://www.katiereus.com

Also, please consider leaving a review at one of your favorite online retailers. It's a great way to help other readers discover new books and I appreciate all reviews.

Happy reading,
Katie

About the Author

KATIE REUS IS THE *USA Today* bestselling author of the Red Stone Security series, the Endgame trilogy and the Redemption Harbor Series. She fell in love with reading at a young age thanks to weekly trips to the library. However, she didn't always know she wanted to be a writer. After changing majors too many times, she finally graduated with a degree in psychology. Not long after that she discovered a new love—writing.

She now spends her days writing paranormal romance and romantic suspense. In addition to writing, she's also obsessed with her dogs, hiking, quilting, and all things aviation.

Booklist

Deadly Ops Series
Targeted · Bound to Danger · Chasing Danger (novella) · Shattered Duty · Edge of Danger · A Covert Affair

Endgame Trilogy
Bishop's Knight · Bishop's Queen · Bishop's Endgame

"Falling for" novellas
Falling for Nola · Falling for Valentine · Falling for Violet

Holiday With a Hitman Series
How the Hitman Stole Christmas · A Very Merry Hitman · All I Want for Christmas is a Hitman

MacArthur Family Series
Falling for Irish · Unintended Target · Saving Sienna

O'Connor Family Series
Merry Christmas, Baby · Tease Me, Baby · It's Me Again, Baby · Mistletoe Me, Baby

***Red Stone Security Series®**

No One to Trust · Danger Next Door · Fatal Deception
Miami, Mistletoe & Murder · His to Protect · Breaking Her Rules
Protecting His Witness · Sinful Seduction · Under His Protection
Deadly Fallout · Sworn to Protect · Secret Obsession
Love Thy Enemy · Dangerous Protector · Lethal Game
Secret Enemy · Saving Danger · Guarding Her
Deadly Protector · Danger Rising · Protecting Rebel

***Redemption Harbor® Series**

Resurrection · Savage Rising · Dangerous Witness
Innocent Target · Hunting Danger · Covert Games · Chasing Vengeance

***Redemption Harbor® Security**

Fighting for Hailey · Fighting for Reese · Fighting for Adalyn
Fighting for Magnolia · Fighting for Berlin · Fighting for Mari · Fighting for Hope

Sanctuary Fall Series

Knight's Storm · Knight's Obsession · Knight's Redemption

***Verona Bay Series**

Dark Memento · Deadly Past · Silent Protector